BOSTON LAW
A Legal Thriller

Boston Law © 2022 by John W. Dennehy.

Macabre Tales Publishing
127 Main Street, Suite 1
Nashua, NH 03060

Written by John W. Dennehy
Cover Design by Wendy Saber Core

First Printed in the United States of America 2022.

BOSTON LAW

A Legal Thriller

John W. Dennehy

Macabre Tales Publishing

CONTENTS

TEN YEARS AGO

PROLOGUE

KENNETH DWYER stood behind the prosecutor's table as the jury filed into the courtroom. They had been out deliberating on the verdict for three days.

He stood facing the judge's bench, but he occasionally glanced over at them.

Each juror looked somber as they stood in front of their seats.

Ken's pulse raced at the thought of winning this highly publicized murder trial. Everyone in Boston had been following it on the news. It would launch his career.

His opposing counsel was a rotund lawyer with a pudgy face from drinking Irish whiskey at the local pubs. Michael Sullivan lingered next to his client, looking more nervous than the guy who stood the chance of spending the rest of his life in prison. The defendant was a local finance guy, married with three children, who was accused of murdering his mistress after she broke off the relationship. A sensational story that had made a splash in the press.

The judge watched the jurors. They fidgeted while a packed courtroom of onlookers stared at them. Judge Maureen Turnbull sat on a high perch, where her oak bench towered over the rest of the courtroom.

The Suffolk County Superior Court featured worn oak tables and chairs. An oak rail barred the well of the courtroom from the pews in the gallery, and it ran in front of the jury box, serving to divide the jury space from the area where the lawyers questioned witnesses.

"Madam Foreperson," the judge said, addressing the woman in the first seat.

The lead juror held a folded slip of paper in her hand.

"Have you reached a verdict?"

"We have, Your Honor."

Judge Turnbull nodded to the bailiff.

The bailiff approached the foreperson and held out his hand.

The foreperson handed the paper over to the bailiff, who carried it to the judge.

She perused the document, then turned her attention back to the foreperson. "What say you?"

"We find the defendant... guilty of second-degree murder."

The judge scanned the rest of the jury. "Was this decision unanimous?"

"Yes," they all said in unison.

Judge Turnbull nodded, satisfied.

She had not taken the time to poll the jurors one at a time, but she wasn't even required to ask them. Ken figured she just wanted to avoid a misstep if the defense lawyer asked for a polling of each juror. Now that each of them had stated as a group the verdict was unanimous, it was less likely one of them would fold under the pressure of speaking alone. The tactic was likely meant to avoid an individual polling altogether.

Turning to Ken Dwyer, the judge said, "Counsel, anything further?"

"The Commonwealth is satisfied with the verdict," Ken replied.

Judge Turnbull looked over to the defense lawyer. "Counsel, is the defense satisfied with the verdict?"

Mickey Sullivan smirked; a nervous tic. "The defense is satisfied that the jury reached a unanimous verdict. However, we do not believe the verdict was correct. I'll be filing a notice of appeal."

"Well, then," Judge Turnbull said, turning to the jury.

The jurors stood with their eyes glued to the trial judge.

"That concludes your service in this matter," she said. "I

know that it was a long trial and you all paid close attention. You are to be commended for your service."

Several jurors nodded in response. A few smiled with appreciation.

"Bailiff, you may escort them out of the courtroom."

He opened a door leading out back, and the jurors filed out for the last time.

Ken exhaled, relieved the case was over and ecstatic with the verdict.

"Great work," he said, turning to Holly Murphy, his second chair counsel.

Holly smiled, and said, "You really pulled this off."

"*We* did it," he said, offering his hand.

She pushed his hand away, opting for a hug instead of a shake.

Ken responded as delicately as possible, then eased away. He smiled at her like a proud mentor, happy to see her share in a major win.

***

AFTER packing up his briefcase, Ken pushed through the mob of onlookers with Holly in tow, trying to get to the door.

A few police officers clapped him on the shoulder and said, "Nice job."

People blocked the way. Courthouse gadflies slowly shuffled towards the door, like movie goers after watching an engaging film. The show was over, and they weren't ready to leave yet. Reporters broke for the lobby, but a few lingered trying to get a word from Ken.

He ignored everyone and kept pushing for the door.

Outside the courtroom, reporters had gathered around waiting for him to comment. People with cameras took pictures. Flashbulbs popped and blinded him. A musty scent of mothballs from the old courthouse mixed with sweat from the anxious crowd and permeated the air.

Ken paused and let Holly catch up, so she could get some exposure.

"Mr. Dwyer," a reporter called. "Are you comfortable with the verdict?"

The question caught him off guard. He gathered himself, and said, "The Commonwealth is satisfied with the verdict. The family suffered a great deal. We are glad to have gotten this result."

"But the case was circumstantial," another reporter said. "Are you sure you got the right guy?"

What is this? Ken thought. He looked at them and nodded.

"Did you expect to win?" shouted a reporter further back.

"Like I've explained, it was a long case. We're glad to see justice done."

"Are you sure justice was done?" the reporter nagged.

"Yes," Ken replied. Then he broke through the throng, heading towards the elevator bank.

Entering a cramped lift with Holly and others, he hit the button for the main lobby and stared at the numbers above the door, as the elevator shook and descended. The approach kept people from asking him further questions.

It was early afternoon and the elevator made it to the lobby without people piling on and off at various floors. When the doors whisked open, Ken pushed his way out and hustled for the exit. His heels clacked across the tile floor, and his heart pounded in his chest.

Other elevator doors opened, and a mob of people made for the door.

Ken stretched out his legs, ambling his long, five-foot and ten-inch frame as fast as he could walk. A few guards in the security area watched him with interest. They knew the drill.

He stepped through the sliding door onto the courthouse steps.

News crews were set up with cameras in the plaza area below.

Ken walked down a couple of the large granite steps and

stopped there. He meant to literally make his statement on the courthouse steps.

Reporters stepped closer, and the cameramen followed suit.

Holly sidled up to Ken. It was time to make a statement and perform damage control.

"Thank you for coming out today," Ken said to everyone. "This was a long and trying ordeal for the victim's family. Make no mistake about it, today justice was done. The District Attorney will perform a press conference tonight."

"Are you satisfied with the verdict?" the closest reporter asked.

Ken nodded. "Absolutely."

The response sounded so sure, the gaggle of reporters just stood there looking surprised.

"Afraid that's all I've got," Ken said. "You can ask questions at the press conference tonight."

He turned and headed up the stairs. "Come on," he whispered to Holly.

At the top of the stairs, he headed down a sidewalk leading away from the plaza area; an escape route. Ken checked over his shoulder and the reporters hadn't followed. They just continued to let the cameras roll with scenes of the courthouse in the background.

"Emmet's pub?" Ken said to Holly.

"Sure."

He reached into a pocket in his suit coat and pulled out a flip phone. Dialing his girlfriend, Alyson Sheehan, he hoped to get through. A busy prosecutor herself, he wondered if she could even take the call.

"Hello," Alyson said, answering on the first ring.

"Guess what?" Ken said.

"You won."

"How did you know?" he asked. "Word couldn't have spread that fast."

"I could tell from your tone," she said, with a flirtatious laugh.

"We're heading over to Emmet's right now. Can you join us?"

"I've got a few things to finish up, but I'll be over soon."

"Okay," Ken said, boyishly. "See you there."

He ended the call and shoved the phone into his pocket. Then he ran a hand through his black hair and grinned. "What a day."

"You can say that again," Holly said.

"What a day," Ken repeated. And it was. He felt a complete adrenaline rush.

They hoofed it down the sidewalk and crossed the far edge of the plaza. And then, they cut through an alley behind the tower located on the corner of Beacon Street. The case would alter his career, but he hadn't a clue just how things would change.

***

ENTERING the Irish pub, Ken was surprised to find that it was already crowded. The place was located near the courthouse and the statehouse, so it had become a local watering hole.

They found a high-top table in the bar area.

Holly climbed onto a chair and hung her bag on the back of it. Ken pulled out a chair slightly and set his briefcase down on the seat. He opted to stand and stretch out his back. After a couple weeks sitting in a courtroom, he didn't feel like sitting on a wooden stool.

"Guess you prefer standing," Holly said.

"Yeah," Ken said. "Two weeks in the courtroom, plus all the time seated at my desk preparing for this trial really did a number on my back."

"I thought you military guys were accustomed to being uncomfortable."

"Well, I was younger then," Ken said with a sly grin.

They both laughed.

She was talking about his service as an infantry officer in the 82nd Airborne Division.

"Honestly, after a trial like this," Ken continued, "all I want to do is hit the gym."

"I hear you on that one. I'm going to yoga before work tomorrow."

A server approached and Holly ordered a cosmopolitan. Ken asked for a gin and tonic. When the server left, Ken cracked a smile.

"What?" Holly said.

"Figured you as a chardonnay type of gal."

"I typically prefer wine. Pinot grigio, though."

"Why the change up?"

Holly's jaw dropped open. "You have to ask? Why to celebrate the biggest trial victory of the year. That's why."

"I'm not sure it's the biggest case of the year."

"Well, it certainly is the most publicized," Holly said. "It was a sensational case. With juicy gossip. And the lack of an eyewitness or a murder weapon made it a difficult trial."

"His DNA was found at the scene."

"That's to be expected. He was dating her."

"You don't buy into this business about him possibly being innocent, do you?"

"No," Holly said. "I'm just saying that it wasn't an easy case."

Ken nodded, feeling relieved. "A close case makes the victory sweeter."

The server returned and placed their drinks on the table. He stared at something beyond Ken before he turned away.

Ken looked to see what had caught the young server's attention.

Alyson had walked into the bar. She wore a black pantsuit, and her lithe body slinked like a cat as she approached. Her black hair was cut slightly above the shoulders, making it long enough to bob and sway with her movements.

Plenty of men in the bar turned their heads to watch her pass by their tables.

At times, Ken wondered what she was doing with him. She had runway model looks.

"Congratulations," Alyson said, kissing him on the cheek.

"Thanks," Ken replied. "You remember Holly?"

"Sure," Alyson said, extending a hand.

"Hi," Holly said, bashfully.

"Congratulations are in order for you as well," Alyson said.

"Why, thank you."

Ken sensed that Alyson's larger than life appearance had set Holly off-kilter. A girl-next-door appearance, Holly was originally from Vermont and didn't have the big city presence like some of the women around town.

Holly looked at Ken, then she looked at Alyson. "You two look a lot alike. Almost twins, except Alyson has brown eyes and Ken has blue."

"People have asked if we were brother and sister before," Ken said. "It's a rather creepy question to hear."

"Sorry, I didn't mean to upset you."

"It's okay," Ken said.

Alyson didn't comment.

There was a lull in the discussion for a bit. Alyson scanned the table. "Aww. You didn't order me a drink," she said to Ken.

"Wasn't sure what you wanted," Ken said, with a shrug.

She frowned. "Chardonnay, like always."

"Wasn't certain," Ken said, trying to dodge the faux pas.

Alyson eyed him suspiciously.

"Holly usually drinks pinot grigio," Ken said, deflecting. "But she's celebrating with a cosmopolitan."

"Honey, it's your victory," Alyson chided him.

"Meaning?"

"I'm not about to add calories to celebrate your win." She smirked.

"Any win of mine is a win for you," Ken said. "We rise up in the boat together."

"This is true." She reached for his drink and took a sip, then put the glass down and grinned mischievously.

The server returned and nervously took Alyson's order.

***

SOON they were settled in, and Alyson had a glass of wine in hand. The place was crawling with prosecutors from their office. Several cops funneled into the bar to join the celebration.

People congratulated them, shook Holly's hand, and slapped Ken on the back.

"There's the man of the hour," lawyers said to Ken, as they filtered into the pub.

Eventually, a group of twenty people surrounded their table. The drinks flowed and people got loose-lipped. Foul language and talking out of school about confidential investigations and cases were plentiful.

Ken stepped away to use the facilities. On his return to the group, he ran into a couple of beat cops who had worked the case. One tall and the other shorter and muscled.

"Nice job counselor," the tall cop said, already half in the bag.

"Thanks," Ken said, angling to step around them.

The other one grabbed his arm. "What about us?" he said, slurring his words.

"Meaning?" Ken replied, wrangling his arm free.

"We congratulate you," the cop snapped in a thick Boston accent. "And you congratulate us. It's a two-way street. A common courtesy that appears lost on you. Winning a case like this isn't all about fancy courtroom theatrics. We pounded the streets. We contributed." The last part came out muttered, barely comprehendible.

"Look," Ken said. "I didn't mean any offense."

"Your mother ever teach you any manners?"

"Guys," Ken said. "Hold up. It's just been a draining couple of weeks. My mind is spent."

"He's got no idea how much we helped him," the tall cop said to his partner.

"What's he talking about?" Ken asked.

"Nothing," the muscular cop said, sheepishly.

"I want to know," Ken demanded.

"It's nothing," the tough cop said, avoiding eye contact.

Ken sensed something serious had gone awry. "What is it?"

"We just took a pass on some evidence," the cop finally admitted. "That's all."

"*Took a pass on some evidence,*" Ken repeated. "What's that even mean?"

"It means that we came across a DNA sample that we never sent on to you," the tall cop said. "No big deal. We got the right guy."

"Another DNA sample?" Ken said. "How come I wasn't told about this?"

They both stood there looking dumbfounded.

"Was it from the defendant?" asked Ken.

"No," the tall cop said.

"Shit." Ken couldn't believe it. They'd failed to turn over exculpatory evidence to the defense. He thought about the development going public. People might speculate that he knew about it, which would be an ethical violation in a highly publicized case. His career could be ruined, or in the least he'd undergo a great deal of scrutiny.

Frustrated, he turned away from them and headed back to his table. Ken sidled up to Alyson and reached for his drink. He took a long swig.

"What's wrong?" she said, furrowing her eyebrows in confusion.

"Something about the case," Ken said, exasperated.

"You already won the case. Let it go."

"Have you seen Dan?"

"Sure, he's right over there," Alyson said, pointing. "He came by looking for you when you were gone. He's quite pleased with the result."

"I'm sure he is."

Ken turned and headed over to find Daniel Collins, the Suffolk County District Attorney. Standing at the corner of the bar, Dan was surrounded by his deputy and a few local politicians. He used every opportunity to gladhand people in hope of climbing higher up the political ladder.

"Hey, Dan," Ken said, cutting into the group.

"There he is, the man of the hour," Dan said with a wide grin.

"Congratulations," the others said almost in unison, partly lifting their glasses in respect.

"Dan," Ken said, anxiously. "We've got to talk."

"What's this about?" Dan asked, looking concerned.

Ken motioned, indicating they should step aside. The two of them found a nook by the bay window overlooking the street.

"What's this about?" Dan said. "You've got me worried."

"You should be worried," Ken said. Then he explained the situation.

"Ken, come on," Dan said. "You can't be serious. That's just a couple of drunk cops talking. Trying to get some recognition in a big case."

"Sounds more serious than that."

"It *sounds* like a load of bull," Dan said, condescendingly. "Something that you could never prove. I suggest you leave it alone. You never *heard* any of this. Heck, *we* never had this discussion."

"Come on, Dan. You know I have to go to the defense with this."

Dan shook his head. "And overturn the biggest case of the year. There would be blow back. It could ruin me. It could ruin *you*. We got the right guy. Now, just let it go."

"But—"

"Forget it!" Dan snapped.

Ken couldn't believe what he was hearing.

Dan peered over Ken's shoulder. "You talk to him," Dan said, then left.

Ken turned and found Alyson standing behind him. She stood there with her arms crossed, and she didn't look pleased.

"Didn't know you were there," Ken said.

"I didn't want to intrude," she said, stepping closer.

"How much did you hear?"

"Enough."

"This is unreal," Ken said. "I can't believe this is happening."

"You have to let it go," Alyson said.

Ken was surprised to hear Alyson suggest that he ignore the buried evidence. "I can't believe you're taking his side," Ken said, shaking his head.

"I'm not. All I want to do is protect you."

"I'm not the one who committed misconduct."

"True. But you'd be tainted by it."

Alyson confirmed Ken's suspicion. His stomach churned with anxiety. Maybe they were right. This was a no-win situation. But he just wasn't wired that way.

She moved closer to him and caressed his face. "Just let it go," she said.

They hugged for a moment.

"I can't," he finally said.

She pulled back. "You'll ruin us."

"It has to be done."

SIX MONTHS LATER

PART ONE

A NEW CLIENT

ONE

KEN DWYER walked down State Street and a cool gust of wind blew through the financial district like a portent of the winter and possible tough times to come.

He wondered where his career was headed and whether he'd made a mistake in reporting the police misconduct in his big case.

Passing in front of a tower with a wide, immaculate sidewalk, he then crossed the street. Ken stepped onto a dilapidated sidewalk, which slanted towards the street at an angle. The concrete had deteriorated from age and road salt. As he walked along, the office buildings were older and smaller.

He approached a limestone building and pushed a plate-glass door open. It was soiled in grime, like the door hadn't been cleaned in years. Stepping into a miniscule lobby, he walked across the shabby tile floor towards the elevator bank.

Inside the timeworn lift, he hit the button to the fourth floor. The lift shook and vibrated as it moved upward. A bell dinged when he reached his floor, and the doors rattled open.

Ken stepped into the suite. Before him were a few desks set in a row without a reception station located between the landing area and the secretarial space. The carpet was bluish green, old and frayed.

His assistant was seated in the last desk, busy typing a pleading. The other desks were empty.

"Good morning, Pat," he said, heading for his office.

"Morning, Ken," she said, smiling without looking up from her work.

He walked past the conference room. It was furnished with a large table, sporting a plastic veneer, which didn't remotely resemble actual wood. A few worn chairs surrounded the table. They had modern wooden arms and a maroon fabric that had seen better days. The lefthand wall sported a built-in bookcase, crammed with outdated reporters and a treatise on Massachusetts legal practice.

Stepping into this office, he took off his tan trench coat and hung it on the back of the door. Then he sat down behind his desk. It was a metal industrial job with a plastic veneer top. A stack of pleadings was piled next to a desktop computer.

A large window overlooked State Street, and a couple laterals housed his files. He heard cars honking at wayward pedestrians on the street below.

Ken loosened his tie, then he fired up the computer and checked his emails. After getting settled in, he worked on an opposition to dismiss a personal injury case. Time flew by and after a couple of hours, he decided to fuel up with some coffee.

He grabbed his coat and headed out. "I'm going to grab a coffee," he said to Pat. "You want anything?"

"I'm good," she replied without looking up.

Ken chuckled. "It's fine if you want me to get you something."

"Got mine on the way in," Pat said, holding up a cup from Dunkin's.

"Okay," he said, stepping into the elevator.

Outside, he stood on the sidewalk waiting for a break in traffic, so he could cross the street. A Dunkin' Donuts was located on the corner with Broad Street.

Michael Sullivan trundled up the sidewalk. "Hey, Ken," he said with a big grin.

"Mickey," Ken replied. "How you doing this morning?"

"I'm doing just fine," Mickey said. "How about we grab some lunch?"

"A little early," Ken said.

Mickey glanced at his watch. "Almost noon. We'll beat the

lunch crowd."

"Sure. Where do you want to go?"

"A place around the corner."

Mickey headed down the sidewalk and Ken followed slightly behind him. The financial district was buzzing with activity. Pedestrians strolled down sidewalks on both sides of the street, heading out to lunch. Cars braked and honked as people darted across the street without using crosswalks. A scent of exhaust wafted through the air.

Several high-rise office buildings were located uphill, with the old state house lingering in the shadows.

Turning the corner at Merchants Row, the street ran the length of a city block then made a ninety-degree turn. An entrance into Faneuil Hall Marketplace was located at the jog in the roadway. A wide, brick walkway cut between a tall building and a restaurant with a solarium roof tucked on the end. The entryway led to a large plaza comprised of cobblestones. In the distance, the brick meeting house stood on the left, and a granite building with columns was located across from it.

As they got closer to the entryway, Ken figured that Mickey was planning on a nice lunch in one of the posh restaurants located in the marketplace. Instead, the pudgy lawyer turned right at a pub and pushed the heavy door open.

Mickey climbed a step to get to an interior door, then pushed it open.

Ken followed him, wondering what the meeting was about.

***

INSIDE, the place resembled many Boston pubs. It had dim lighting, a few brick walls, plank floors, a large bar in the center, and high-top tables surrounding the bar area. Flatscreen televisions were hung about the establishment, broadcasting local sports and highlights.

"Come on," Mickey said. "Let's grab a table."

They found a wooden table pushed against an inner wall.

Ken pulled out a stool, then he took off his coat and hung it on the back of the chair. He sat down and reached for a menu.

The scent of spilt beer floated up from the floor.

Mickey climbed onto a stool and chuckled.

"What?" asked Ken.

"A couple things," Mickey replied. "First, you probably thought we were headed to a nice restaurant in Faneuil Hall."

"That crossed my mind on the way over here," Ken admitted.

"We don't stand on ceremony in this business," Mickey said, amused. "Every penny that gets spent on expenses comes out of someone's pocket. In this case, my pocket. We're not like the big firms with a budget to spend on meals and entertainment. Budgets I might add, which are for the partners and come from the labor of the associates and staff."

Ken nodded. "Understood."

"The second point is this," Mickey continued. "You don't need a menu here. This is a burger and fries place. The food is good. But I wouldn't venture into the realms of salmon and chicken salad."

They both laughed.

Then the server approached. She set down a Jameson's Irish whiskey on the rocks in front of Mickey.

"Sandra," Mickey said. "I'll go with the usual."

She nodded, then looked at Ken.

"I'll get the same as him. Burger and fries."

"What will you have to drink?" she asked.

"Diet cola," Ken said.

She jotted down his order. Then she went over to the galley and turned in the slip for the cook. Sandra returned to her station and began refilling drinks for people scattered around the bar.

"So, what's the occasion?" Ken said.

Mickey took a sip of his drink. His nose and cheeks were already red.

Ken couldn't tell if it was the cold weather, or if Mickey drank more than he initially had thought. He watched the man take another sip of whiskey.

Then, Mickey looked at him and grinned. "It's about this," Mickey said, patting his coat. He pulled out an envelope from an inner breast pocket.

"I don't follow."

"Remember our agreement when I took you on?" Mickey said.

"Yeah."

"I agreed to pay you a salary of what you were making at the D.A.'s Office, plus a third of whatever came in on any file that you were working on."

"Sure. That's the deal."

"Well, it turns out that you're a real ball buster."

Ken looked at him askance.

Mickey laughed and took a long swig from his drink. He wiped his mouth with the back of a hand and said, "I've decided to sweeten the deal a bit."

"Mickey, you don't have to do that," Ken said.

"I know. But I want to." Mickey placed the envelope in front of Ken.

The envelope was transparent enough that Ken could see there was a check inside.

"You settled three personal injury cases for a lot more than I had projected," Mickey said. "So, I took the fee that I had anticipated, and the rest is yours."

"Mickey, you really don't have to do this."

Sandra returned with their lunches and slid the plates in front of them.

Mickey polished off his glass, rattled the cubes around, and took a final sip. "This calls for another," he said to Sandra.

She smiled, looked at Ken and said, "Must be quite a day."

As Sandra left to fetch the next drink, Mickey leaned forward and grabbed his burger. He took a large bite, then sat back, savoring the beef. "This," he said, pointing at his plate, "is the best burger in town. And it goes quite well with a Jameson's."

Ken took a bite of his burger. "It's good."

Sandra returned and set Mickey's drink down. Then she placed a soft drink in front of Ken.

Mickey smiled at her. "Much appreciated," he said.

After Sandra left, Mickey turned serious. "You've done great work on those cases," he said. "But make no mistake about it, the money from run-of-the-mill personal injury cases is peanuts. We pay our regular overhead through the criminal defense cases, which are billed on an hourly rate. The car accident cases end up paying salary."

"Okay," Ken said. "I'm following."

"The real money comes from contingency fee cases where you can get to deep pockets," Mickey said, with a twinkle in his eyes. "I've got a case where a state trooper chased a car and the fleeing car lost control and hit a bunch of kids who were standing in front of a public school."

Ken cringed at the thought of kids being seriously injured or killed.

"The kids all survived," Mickey said, assuaging Ken's concerns.

"So, what's the case about?" asked Ken.

"I'm suing the trooper for negligence, the fleeing car for negligence," Mickey explained, gesticulating. "The best part of the case arises from a recent renovation project to the school. The engineer didn't specify the correct bollards, and the contractor didn't install them correctly."

Ken wasn't sure how all this connected.

"We have a negligent construction claim against the contractor and a professional liability claim against the engineer." Mickey sat back beaming. "The contractor has deep pockets and possibly some insurance coverage. The engineering firm has professional liability coverage. Those policies have the big limits."

"So, do you want me to jump in on that case?" Ken asked, canting his head.

"No," Mickey replied. "At least not yet. I'm merely explaining to you how these cases can play out. This is kind of your pocket

MBA in law firm management."

Ken nodded. "I follow you."

"Good." Mickey took a long sip from his drink, then he set the glass down.

"This was a nice gesture," Ken said, indicating to the envelope.

Mickey shook has head. "It's not a gesture."

Ken stared at him, puzzled.

"That," Mickey said, pointing to the envelope. "That is an investment. And it's an incentive."

Ken smiled. "Afraid you'll have to explain."

"The investment comes like this," Mickey said. "Buy yourself a couple new suits and get rid of those polyester blends. You look like a prosecutor, or an insurance defense lawyer."

"I thought a conservative look would help."

Mickey nodded. "It will. Just do it with a wool blended suit."

"Okay. What else?"

"Get out of that dive in Brighton. Buy yourself a condo downtown near the office."

Ken glanced at the envelope, wondering how much money was in there. "And the second part?" Ken said. "The incentive?"

"That's what I like about you," Mickey said, cackling. "You never miss a beat."

"And?"

"The incentive is this," Mickey said. "I'm putting you on a new case. You'll run it out. There's an hourly criminal piece to it, and there's potentially a civil rights case. That's one where you can collect your fees if you win, so bill them as you go."

"How big is the case?" Ken asked.

Mickey shrugged. "Who cares?"

Ken shook his head, bewildered by the comment.

Mickey smiled, kindly. "Listen, kid. You're an exceptional lawyer. You have courtroom presence. And you move around like a lawyer on television, not like the rest of us. It takes a special kind of memory and self-confidence to pull off what you do…"

"But?"

"You've got a heck of a lot to learn." Mickey ate a few fries. "You recover $10,000 on a case like this, and you get your legal fees on top of it. So, if the verdict is ten grand or a hundred grand, it doesn't matter. The legal fees could run a hundred and fifty to two hundred and fifty thousand."

Ken sat back. He didn't realize such cases were out there.

"I'm busy with the school crash case," Mickey said. "You run this one out alone. If you chalk up a good fee, I'll split it with you on a fifty-fifty basis."

TWO

LATER that afternoon, Ken was busy at his desk when he heard the elevator doors rattle open. A moment later Pat stood at the threshold to his office.

"Your new client is here," she said. "Should I lead him into the conference room?"

"No," Ken said, rising from his chair. "I'll take care of it."

"You've got it then," Pat said, flashing a knowing smile before turning away.

"Thanks, Pat," Ken said, stepping from his office into the hall running alongside the reception area.

Ken turned to the landing in front of the elevators to see what had caused Pat to grin.

Trevor Belliveau stood before him looking every part of a two-bit thug. He wore designer jeans that had seen some mileage. Belliveau's long-sleeved t-shirt was covered with maroon bedazzled buttons sewn to the fabric, as if trying to fashion a bird of prey. Ken couldn't tell if it was an eagle or a falcon, but the getup revealed a young man who had logged in a lot of hours at nightclubs and trendy bars.

Belliveau had short, dirty blonde hair, as if he was trying to hide a thinning hairline. His beady, hazel eyes projected an underlying intensity. The kid's wiry body had some muscularity, and he didn't seem like someone who could stay put for very long.

He had three days of stubble, reflecting the outline of a burgeoning beard. Ken figured Belliveau spent a lot of time in front of a mirror with a trimmer keeping it that way.

"Good afternoon," Ken said, stepping towards his new client. Belliveau nodded and uttered a grunt.

"I'm Ken Dwyer," the lawyer said, extending a hand.

"Trevor Belliveau," the kid said, grasping Ken's hand tightly.

The kid held Ken's hand longer than necessary and squeezed it hard, as if he were trying desperately to hurt Ken and intimidate him at the same time.

Ken inhaled and let the moment pass. Belliveau let go and smirked.

"This way," Ken said, motioning to the conference room.

"Sure," Belliveau said, gruffly.

Ken stepped inside and Belliveau strutted into the room. Then, Ken shut the door, knowing that he already detested the man.

THREE

SETTLING into the conference room, Belliveau took a seat near the door with his back to the bookcase. Ken grabbed a notepad from a cabinet located near the window, then he sat down across from the new client.

"We need to go through some preliminary information," Ken said.

"Sure," Belliveau replied. "Whatever you need."

Ken noticed the kid had placed a next generation phone on the table. Having only purchased a flip phone recently, Ken couldn't believe this young man already had the latest technology.

"Let's start with your arrest," Ken said. "How did it go down?"

"Didn't Mickey fill you in on all of this?" Belliveau said, sounding annoyed.

Ken frowned. "Well, I need to hear it from you."

"Sure," Belliveau said. "I'm going through a divorce, so I stay with my aunt at her house in Lynn. It's a double decker near English High School. The place is like the triple-deckers you see around Boston, only it's two-stories instead of three."

"I get the picture," Ken said, nodding.

"She lives on the first floor because she is older, and it's easier for her to get in and out."

"What about you? Where do you stay?"

"I live on the second level," Belliveau said, sounding cheery.

"Does she have access to the second level?"

"Yeah," Belliveau said, sounding miffed like it had been a

stupid question. "It's her house. But there are two separate apartments, with kitchens and bathrooms in each one. I come and go as I please, just like any other tenant with an apartment."

"Is there a lease?"

Belliveau sat there for a moment. "Might be," he finally said.

"There is, or there isn't," Ken said. "Which is it?"

"To tell you the truth, I'm not exactly sure. I'll have to check on that."

"As you sit there today, you don't know for sure?"

"Whose side are you on?" Belliveau snapped.

Ken looked at the kid and grinded his teeth, while studying the arrogant young man. "Listen, we need to know the facts in order to determine the possible defenses and what steps to take in a case. And we need accurate information. We can't assume anything. The worst thing you can do is take a position in a criminal case and find out that you cannot support it. Doing so has a way of blowing up on you at trial."

Belliveau nodded. "So, you're just being thorough?"

"Yes."

"I can't remember if there is a lease or not," Belliveau said. "See, I've lived in that apartment on and off for about a decade."

"How old are you?"

"Twenty-eight," Belliveau said, grinning as he crossed his arms.

"Do you pay rent?" asked Ken.

"Not really."

Ken glanced at the kid askance.

"Well," Belliveau muttered. "I give her money for the oil bill. Pay the electric. And I give her money towards her groceries. Stuff like that."

He initially came across as a little nervous. Now, he sounded proud of himself. It seemed like he saw it as an accomplishment just because he sent a little money his aunt's way. Belliveau didn't seem to register that she could rent the apartment to someone and get double or triple what he was paying her. Ken got the feeling Belliveau took his aunt for granted. The kid might even think he was entitled to free rent.

Ken took notes as they went along. It wasn't as cut and dried as Mickey had let on. The kid clearly thought he had solid defenses, though.

"So, what happened?" Ken asked, looking up from his notes.

"What happened is this," Belliveau said. "I was out, and the police came by without a warrant. They asked my aunt if they could search my apartment. She told them they could. And here I am."

"What were they looking for?"

"Prescription drugs."

"Why?"

Belliveau shrugged. "You'd have to ask them."

"Well, I'm asking you," Ken snapped. "The police don't divulge their motives to criminal defense lawyers."

"They got it into their heads that I steal prescription drugs and sell them."

"Why do they think that?"

"Beats me," the kid said, raising his hands.

"Did they find any prescription drugs?" asked Ken.

"No," Belliveau said, emphatically.

"What did they find?"

"Nothing in the apartment."

"Why were you arrested?" Ken said.

"They found some pry bars in the basement," Belliveau said.

"Pry bars?"

"Yeah. Pry bars and a few other items like that."

"What kind of items?" Ken asked, while taking notes.

"Hacksaws, drills, cutting tools."

"Anything else?"

"Might have been a hammer and a nail setter."

"What was the charge?"

"Conspiracy to burglarize a pharmacy," Belliveau said, cracking a sarcastic grin, like the entire situation was ridiculous.

"Did they suggest these items were used for breaking into a pharmacy to steal prescription drugs?" Ken said.

"Yes."

"What's your explanation for these items?"

"Construction work," Belliveau said, with an arrogant tone.

Ken looked the kid over. Belliveau had a fairly light complexion; no sign of working in the sun appeared anywhere on the man. Thinking back to the handshake, the kid lifted weights and had strength, but his hands were soft.

"You use the items in construction work?" Ken finally said.

Belliveau nodded and smiled. "Yeah. I do."

"Do you have any documents to back that up?" Ken said. "Invoices, project documents?"

"Invoices?" Belliveau waved a hand, flippantly.

"We need to know how well we can support your position."

"Might," Belliveau added. "I don't keep a lot of that."

"How do you pay your taxes?"

"My wife tended to handle that stuff. It was mostly subcontractor work."

"Meaning?"

"I'd work on a job and get paid. End of story."

Ken nodded, understanding.

"Besides," the kid added. "I haven't done that work in a while. Not since my wife and I split up a couple years ago."

"What do you do now?"

The kid didn't respond. He sat there, staring at Ken.

"You seem upset," Ken said.

"No," Belliveau said, but he was fuming.

"You appear ready to explode."

"No. I'm fine." But he didn't look fine.

"You still haven't answered the question…"

"I do a little of this, and a little of that. I get by."

"What kind of prescriptions do they think you were stealing?"

"Oxycontin." The smug demeanor was back.

"Listen, we're going to have to roundtable this," Ken said. "If we decide to move forward, we'll get you an—"

"Whoa. Whoa!" Belliveau snapped.

"Engagement letter."

"No. No," Belliveau said, shaking his head.

"What?" Ken said. "This is the process."

"No," Belliveau complained. "Mickey said you were taking the criminal case, and you'd sue those cops for violating my rights."

"That's not how it works," Ken said, sitting back.

"No," Belliveau repeated. "No way."

"I don't know what to tell you."

"You work for Mickey," Belliveau said, pointing at Ken. "And he works for me. We've got an arrangement."

"Like I was saying—"

"No!" Belliveau abruptly stood up. His chair rolled back and hit the bookcase.

"This really isn't a way to begin an attorney/client relationship," Ken said. "You might want to consider..."

"I ain't considering nothing."

"Suit yourself."

"Nope," Belliveau said, belligerently.

He fished a hand into the threadbare front pocket of his designer jeans, while shaking his head. Irritation reflected in his wild eyes. Then he pulled out a wad of cash. Belliveau unfolded the bundle of money and flipped through it, counting out crisp notes.

"There you go," Belliveau said, setting a bunch of fresh bills on the table.

"We can't take a retainer without an executed engagement letter."

"It's done all the time. Go to any district court and there are lawyers hanging around who will represent you. You pay them five hundred bucks and they go into a hearing and serve as your counsel."

"Afraid we don't operate that way."

"Take the money," Belliveau said. "I'll talk to Mickey about the rest."

Ken stood up. "I'm not your lawyer without a signed engagement letter."

"Mickey can get it. And one for the lawsuit against the police," Belliveau said, heading for the door.

FOUR

KEN heard the elevator doors close, then he left the conference room and marched down the hall towards Mickey's office.

Pat looked up but didn't say anything. She appeared taken aback.

Ken figured that she'd heard Belliveau storm out. He knew he should just head into his office and calm down. But he was far too upset to let it go, even for an hour.

Reaching the corner office, he found the door ajar.

He rapped on the door and entered the spacious room.

Mickey was sitting behind a huge desk, engrossed in some paperwork. He looked up and smiled. Then he registered Ken's anger and looked confused. And then he seemed perturbed. "What do you need?" Mickey said, sounding annoyed.

It seemed as though he didn't care what had gotten Ken upset. Whatever it was, Mickey simply didn't want to hear it. Ken wondered if he'd made a mistake by interrupting him.

"We need to talk about this new case," Ken said, stepping into the room.

"Sure. Take a seat," Mickey said, indicating to a chair.

Ken looked at the two plush leather chairs situated in front of Mickey's desk. He opted for the one the senior lawyer had pointed to. Ken sat down and looked at Mickey.

"What's the issue?" Mickey said.

"The criminal and civil cases turn on whether the search was authorized."

"And?"

"The owner of the property authorized the search."

"No warrant," Mickey said, shaking his head.

"They don't need one if the person who owns and controls the property authorizes the search," Ken said, pedantically.

Mickey grinned. "You sound like a prosecutor talking."

"Shouldn't I think like one?"

"No." Mickey shrugged. "Look around."

Ken scanned the room. Aside from a small space displaying Mickey's law degree from Boston College, the walls were adorned with framed newspaper articles. The lawyer's big verdicts.

"Those cases were won by outthinking the prosecutors and insurance defense lawyers," Mickey said, proudly.

"But to outthink them, don't I have to know where they're coming from?"

"Sure. At first."

Ken thought about the comment.

"Plan on how to win, Kenny. Don't focus on how to destroy your own case."

"The prospective client had his own dedicated space. An apartment."

"That's good," Mickey said.

"But the police didn't find any contraband in the apartment."

"Why did they make the arrest?"

"They found tools used for pharmacy break-ins. But the items were in the basement, which is not part of Belliveau's dedicated space."

Mickey shook his head.

"What?"

"First, since when is it illegal to own tools?"

"The charge is conspiracy to burglarize—"

"Stop," Mickey said, holding up a hand. "Don't care. You're thinking like a prosecutor. Maybe you should start with a premise that you don't trust the police."

Ken stared at him, wondering where this was going.

"Look, if the police had anything to support that charge, they would have gotten a warrant," Mickey explained. "They didn't have anything, so they went fishing around the house. They got the lowdown on the elderly aunt and took a stab at it."

"And?"

"They came up with nothing."

"Well, they got the tools."

"The tools are worthless without anything else."

"Why even make the arrest? Why not go away empty handed, rather than attempt to prosecute a charge that won't stick?"

Mickey's eyes lit up. "Those are the types of questions that you should ask yourself," Mickey said, leaning forward with excitement.

"Meaning?"

"They made the arrest for a couple of reasons," Mickey replied. "They wanted to see if they could shake the tree. Make an arrest. Get someone into the station. See if they'd talk."

"And the other reason?"

"Leverage to avoid a lawsuit."

Ken nodded, understanding. Police officers didn't always operate to seek a conviction. Sometimes there are other motives for their actions.

"We through?" asked Mickey.

"No. This discussion was all about the arrest based on the tools."

"So?"

"You sounded like there were two points about the search," Ken said.

Mickey sat back, ruminating. "Sure," he said after a moment. "Aside from the fact that the search resulted in seizure of legally owned tools, you need to delve into the facts with the client further."

"How so?"

"Form an argument that the tools were in a dedicated space. That way, they would be subject to protection from unlawful search and seizure."

"How so?"

"There are a string of college roommate and crash pad type

cases," Mickey said. "The police get a warrant or authorization to search one person's possessions. They go into the closet of a roommate and find weed or whatever. The search is illegal because it deals with another person's dedicated space, who had an expectation of privacy."

A light went off in Ken's head. And he realized the power of experience.

FIVE

BACK at his desk, Ken picked up the phone and called Trevor Belliveau. The phone rang twice and Belliveau answered.

"Hello," Belliveau said, with a cautious tone.

"Trevor, this is Ken Dwyer here."

"What's up?" Belliveau said. "You talk to Mickey?"

"Yes, I did," Ken replied.

"Figured. So, we're all set?" The kid sounded cocky, like he thought he had something hanging over Ken's head, an in with the boss.

"We're going to need a little more information," Ken said.

"Like what?" Now he sounded miffed.

Ken paused before taking it any further. He could hear wind gusts, which interrupted the reception. Belliveau was clearly outside.

"Are you in a secure location?" Ken asked.

"Sure," Belliveau said. "Just stepped outside of a convenience store on Union Street. Nobody's around."

"Tell me a little bit about where these tools were stored in the basement."

"There was a corner in the basement near the bulkhead where I kept all my stuff…"

"All your stuff?"

"Yeah. Like I've told you, I have lived there on an off for a decade."

"And?"

"There's a corner where I keep all my stuff," Belliveau said.

"What kind of stuff?"

"This important?"

"Could be."

"I've got weights, an exercise bike, and a rowing machine down there," Belliveau said, sounding enthusiastic, as if he was catching on to the importance of a dedicated space.

"What else?"

"There are plastic boxes with my taxes and business records."

"What about the tools?"

"I kept the tools in a storage locker."

"Where is the storage locker?"

"Like I've told you. It was in the area near the bulkhead."

"Describe the area."

"The bulkhead was in the back lefthand corner of the house. All my stuff was kept in the back righthand corner of the basement. There was a travel lane, so to speak, running from the bulkhead towards the front of the house. My stuff was just to the right of the bulkhead on the back wall, and all of my stuff filled an area from the travel lane to the righthand wall. I'd say it ran about sixteen feet by ten feet."

"Did your aunt keep any of her stuff in that place?" asked Ken.

"Heavens no." Belliveau suddenly went from being crass to talking like an uppity Bostonian. It sounded phony.

"We have to photograph that space immediately."

"Sure. I can take care of it."

"This would be better handled if I were present," Ken said.

"Is that necessary?"

"Yes."

"Okay. But I can't do it right now."

"When can you be there?"

Belliveau did not respond. There was a pause in the discussion, like he was trying to think of an excuse. Wind rattled over the line. Ken heard a few cars drive past.

"I've got an appointment. I can meet you there in a couple of hours."

"Fine. I'll bring the engagement letters for you to sign."

"Great." And Belliveau suddenly sounded happy.

"We might want to get an affidavit from your aunt," Ken said.

"No way!"

"Why not? It could help."

"She's old," Belliveau said, almost pleading.

"We can talk to her, then my office will draft it. She'd only have to review and sign."

"I really don't want to involve her in this," Belliveau insisted.

"Your aunt is already involved."

"I doubt this is going very far. We'll involve her only if necessary."

"Having her—"

"Like I said… keep her out of this."

Ken thought about it. The client had the final say on something like this. All he could do was offer the best course of action. He'd keep careful notes about every discussion with this client and use them later if something went wrong.

"All right," Ken finally said. "Let's get together this afternoon."

SIX

DRIVING north that afternoon, Ken ran into light traffic on his way to Belliveau's place.

The sun shined bright off the windshield of his aging Volkswagen Jetta. He'd bought the car when he joined the 82nd Airborne Division out of college as a second lieutenant. A decal with jump wings was plastered on the rear window.

Exiting the highway, he drove down a road that wound along a reservoir. A couple of swans and a few ducks swam in the choppy water. He thought about how Belliveau didn't want his aunt to sign an affidavit. It was an unusual position to take. Most criminal defendants lean heavily on family members to keep them out of prison.

The guy is bad news, Ken thought.

He turned onto Chestnut Street, a main throughfare lined with older multifamily homes and commercial establishments. There were barber shops, liquor stores, and convenience stores scattered between the two-story clapboard houses and triple-deckers. The corner stores boasted the sale of lottery tickets, and the windows were covered with advertisements for various brands of cigarettes. Scraps of paper littered the sidewalk.

Lynn was a rundown city that had seen better days.

Turning onto Goodridge Street, he drove past the high school built in the 1890s. It was comprised of limestone and brick and had two large pillars flanking the front entrance. Ken made a left onto a quaint residential street and checked the numbers on the front doors.

Most of the houses found in this turn-of-the-century

44

neighborhood were well maintained and in good condition. Sidewalks ran down both sides of the street, with maple trees growing from the small tracks of grass running along the roadway. It looked like it hadn't changed much since the houses were built. The majority of the dwellings were two-story homes, packed in tight with a driveway leading to small backyards. Few houses had a garage.

Ken knew the neighborhood well. He'd walked along those sidewalks as a boy.

The house where Ken had lived until the age of five was located on the lefthand side of the street. Ken scanned the righthand side of the road, looking for Belliveau's place. He spotted it halfway up the block from his old house.

A double-decker in decent shape, it had a front porch on both levels. Two front doors were located off the first-floor porch.

Ken was familiar with the approach. The door on the left opened into an apartment on the first floor and the door to the right led to a minuscule hallway with a tight staircase winding up to an apartment on the next level.

There was a black Chevy Malibu parked in the narrow driveway.

Ken pulled in behind the Chevy and climbed out of his car. The temperature felt warmer, so he left his trench coat on the back seat. He stretched out his back, then he ascended the front stairs and walked across the porch to the door on the right.

Pressing the doorbell, he didn't hear a ring. Ken knocked on the door and waited. Nothing.

He rang the other doorbell, wondering if the aunt was home. It rang, but nobody came to greet him. Given that there was only one car in the driveway, he figured the aunt was out running errands.

Ken thought about why he was meeting the client at the house.

Stepping down from the porch, Ken walked down the driveway and headed around to the back of the house. The dwelling was set on fieldstone basement walls, which protruded above the ground about three feet.

A couple of basement windows were situated along the driveway side of the house. The window towards the rear of the house was cast in a shadow from the house next door. Light from a hanging bulb in the basement illuminated the window.

Ken peeked inside. Belliveau was in the cellar, possibly moving boxes around.

Walking briskly, Ken made his way to the end of the house. A cement walkway led to a stoop with a backdoor at the top of the stairs. Ken planned to knock on the door and get Belliveau's attention, then he noticed a bulkhead with the doors propped open.

Ken approached the bulkhead, then looked down into the dank basement.

Just beyond the bottom of the stairs, he found Belliveau. The kid stood in the shadows looking up at him.

Belliveau mounted the stairs and ascended them quickly.

He rushed out onto the dried lawn and Ken took a step backward. A wild gleam reflected in the young man's eyes.

"You aren't supposed to be here for another forty minutes," Belliveau said.

"Light traffic," Ken offered.

"What? Are you checking up on me?" Belliveau said, bunching his fists.

Ken noticed beads of sweat dripping from Belliveau's forehead.

Belliveau stepped closer. "I asked you a question."

Adrenaline rushed up Ken's spine. Every muscle in his body grew tense with anticipation of a conflict. "You need to step back," Ken said sternly.

Recognition of his improper conduct registered in Belliveau's eyes. The intensity shifted to a look of concern. "Sorry," he said, stepping away. "You surprised me. That's all."

Ken figured it was something more. "Were you moving anything around?"

Belliveau turned to Ken, looking peeved. "No."

"Are you sure?"

"Go take a look for yourself."

"Think I'll do that."

"Sure. But you might want to look at this first," Belliveau said. Fishing a folded paper from the back pocket of his threadbare designer jeans, he handed it over to Ken.

"What's this?" Ken said, taking the document.

"The lease. See, I had to have one in order to register my car."

Ken took a quick look at the document, then shoved it into an inner suit coat pocket. "Let's take a look," he said, descending the stairs.

The basement was rectangular. A couple of overhead lights illuminated the cramped space. It was cluttered with boxes and discarded belongings the kid's aunt couldn't bear to part with. The cellar was musty, and the foundation built from fieldstones probably leaked in the springtime.

Ken scanned the place for an area of demarcation.

"My stuff is on that carpeted area," Belliveau said, as if reading Ken's mind.

To the left of the bulkhead entryway, there was a large piece of soiled tan carpet. It measured about fourteen feet by fourteen feet. Boxes were neatly arranged on the carpet. Some were translucent plastic and packed with business records.

A weight bench was stranded in the middle. Dumbbells and plates were scattered among the boxes. There was an exercise bike and a rowing machine, just like the kid had said. The area had likely been set up as a workout location years beforehand. Now, the equipment was dusty and some of the weights were rusted.

Ken noticed a metal storage locker against the wall. "Is this where the tools were kept?"

"Yup," Belliveau replied, stepping to the locker.

Belliveau opened the metal doors and the hinges creaked.

Inside, there were shelves on one side and a large space on the other. A few tools remained in the locker: a shovel, a toolbelt, a reciprocating saw, and a box of wrenches. Several glass jars were filled with nuts and bolts, like the kind a grandfather would keep in a basement or garage.

"They didn't take everything," Belliveau said.

Scanning the basement again, Ken said, "You sure you didn't move anything?"

"Definitely."

"You know the police usually photograph a crime scene. If you present photographs at a hearing and the conditions are changed, they'll know it."

"I didn't move a thing," Belliveau said. And he sounded cocksure.

"Okay, then." Ken reached into his pocket and pulled out his phone. "Go ahead and photograph this area with my phone."

SEVEN

SITTING on a dingy sofa in his tiny apartment in Brighton, Ken and Alyson dug into takeout from a nearby Chinese restaurant.

The place resembled a pad occupied by college kids. Used furniture, an old television, and bare walls gave the place a run-down feel. It seemed like a temporary residence, but Ken had lived there since law school.

"You're awfully quiet," Alyson said.

"This new client has me on edge."

She reached for her glass of red wine, located on the coffee table. Taking a long sip, it seemed like a delay tactic used to prepare for something important she planned to say. A lawyer's trick done at trial.

"If you're about to say that you told me so," Ken said. "Touché."

"Well, I told you so."

"Prosecutors don't get to pick their clients," Ken said. "You have crotchety police officers, corrupt cops, dumb officers who make mistakes. Sometimes the victims or their families are hard to deal with."

"Sure. But you *get* to nab the bad guys."

"The longer I'm in this, the more I wonder who *are* the bad guys."

"Now you're questioning the police because of one bad experience that you had," Alyson said, shaking her head.

"It's more than that. This case involves some very questionable police conduct."

"Like what?"

"They arrested the guy for having tools."

"What kind of tools?"

"Pry bars."

"What's the charge?"

"Conspiracy to burglarize pharmacies."

Alyson nodded, completely understanding the situation. "The police rushed to make an arrest. Sounds like you've got a good case. What's the problem?"

"I don't trust the guy," Ken said, leaning forward scoping out the carton of brown rice.

"Well, he is a criminal defendant. Makes sense not to trust him."

"Just wonder if I'm being too paranoid," Ken said. "I've doubted him on a few things, and he might have been playing it straight with me."

"That goes with the territory. *Criminal defense.*" She spoke it like a bad word.

"Maybe."

"So, what's the deal with this guy?"

Ken wanted to explain, but he knew he couldn't get into any specifics. "You're a prosecutor. I've already said enough."

"Suit yourself." Alyson turned back to the television.

Glancing around the apartment, Ken thought about the check that Mickey had given him. It was equal to a year's salary as a prosecutor, and he was getting paid the same salary as when he was a prosecutor. "It pays the bills, though," Ken said.

Alyson spun towards him. "*That* kind of money is irrelevant," she snapped.

"How so?" Ken really wondered where she was going with this.

"You can buy shiny new things. But you cannot buy prominence."

Ken ruminated over her comment for a bit, wondering exactly what she meant. "You're embarrassed of me. Aren't you?" he finally said, jumping to the conclusion.

"No," she replied. But she broke off eye contact.

"You'd prefer that I stayed at the D.A.'s Office," he said.

Alyson nodded. "Yes. But I can understand your desire to make a move."

"Just not to a small shop on State Street."

"You're an exceptional lawyer," she said. "If you stayed at the D.A.'s Office, you would have moved up in the ranks. You could have launched a career in politics. Maybe landed a job at a bigger firm."

Everything she said made sense. But it wasn't him. Ken couldn't see himself doing any of those things. "Maybe I don't want to go into politics," he said after a moment. "I like being a trial lawyer. The D.A.'s Office doesn't pay the bills and most lawyers at the big firms spend all their time working long hours, just pushing paper around."

"So, where does that leave you?" Her question was pointed and sounded critical.

"My hope was to get experience and run my own firm."

"You're just an associate in a very *small* firm."

"I'll get there. And it won't take long." He grinned thinking about the check.

She considered him carefully. "You won't have any power or prestige."

"Those things don't pay the bills."

"You shouldn't confuse power with money. In this town, you can garner a lot of power without making much money."

"I just don't see how you can live off power."

She smirked condescendingly. "Guess you'll never know."

PART TWO

SUPPRESSION HEARING

EIGHT

A FEW WEEKS later, Ken hustled around a crowded courthouse looking for Belliveau. They had an afternoon hearing on a motion to suppress all evidence obtained from the search.

The Essex County Superior Court was located in a new building with wide hallways and soaring ceilings. It had plenty of glass, resembling modern architecture. The place housed numerous types of courts on various floors. Ken wondered if he'd find Belliveau in time.

A lawyer functions under a lot of stress while performing at trials and hearings. One of the biggest pressure points is worrying about key witnesses and clients showing up for court. When the client is late for a hearing, it distracts their attorney and takes away from last minute preparation time.

Finally, he spotted Belliveau sauntering down the courthouse hallway. The kid wore a suit like you might see on a businessman. The suit coat was unbuttoned, and Ken noticed that Belliveau wore a wide, brown leather belt with a large buckle. It was the type of belt you might see worn with a pair of Wrangler jeans. Belliveau wore shiny, brown loafers. The shoes were something one might expect to see in a nightclub.

"Where have you been?" Ken griped.

"Relax," Belliveau said. "I ran into a little traffic."

"That's why I told you to leave early."

"Sure. But I also had to make a stop at Dunkin's," Belliveau said, grinning.

Ken shook his head. "I'm not certain you're taking this seriously enough," he said.

"Sure I am."

"If this hearing doesn't go well, the prosecutor is going to ask the judge to revoke your bail. You could go away in handcuffs."

Belliveau cracked a grin. "You kidding me? The jail is full of criminals. Ain't no way a judge is sending me to the slammer for owning a few tools... used in my trade."

Ken couldn't believe what he was hearing. The kid was cocky. *Are they all like this,* he thought. *Maybe Alyson was right.*

NINE

STEPPING into a packed courtroom, Ken noticed the judge had already taken the bench. A hearing was in progress and two lawyers stood at counsel tables, while the judge rooted through a file.

Ken wondered if they had already done a roll call. He spotted an open space in the gallery and headed over to the pew.

"Slip in there," he whispered to Belliveau.

The kid shrugged and took a seat, bumping into the person next to him.

Ken took off his overcoat and placed it on the pew. As he eased in beside his client, the judge glanced up from his file and glowered at Ken.

"Nice of you to join us this morning," said Judge Cortland Mathers, III, sounding peeved by the interruption.

Ken flashed an apologetic smile, then searched the courtroom, trying to discern the prosecutor for his case. The new courthouse had lofty ceilings and a spacious gallery. He saw various prosecutors and police officers, as well as defense lawyers and their clients.

He noticed the Essex County District Attorney seated in a plush chair on the other side of the bar. Ken figured one of the matters before the court must be important enough to bring the lead prosecutor down from his ivy tower. A younger lieutenant from the D.A.'s Office was seated next to him. Ken recognized the second chair lawyer from local events, but he couldn't recall his name.

Somehow, in just a brief time, the kid had gone from a

nobody to the District Attorney's righthand man.

The judge addressed the two lawyers before him. "I'll take this under advisement and will issue an order soon," he said. "Thank you for coming in today."

While the lawyers packed up, the sessions clerk rose from his table adjacent to the bench and walked towards Ken. "Are you here for the Belliveau matter?"

Ken partially stood up. "Yes."

"Thank you," the clerk said, turning away.

The clerk walked towards the well of the courtroom, nodded to the judge, then he turned and faced the gallery. "The next matter before the court is Commonwealth versus Belliveau."

Ken stood up. "Wait here," he said to Belliveau.

Pushing his way through the gate, he noticed the District Attorney rise from his chair and move towards the prosecutor's table, which is located closer to the jury box. The younger lawyer accompanied him to the table. Two prosecutors for a routine hearing, and one of them was the District Attorney himself.

What is this? Ken thought. *The crime of the century.*

TEN

STANDING at their respective counsel tables, Ken and the prosecutors quietly waited for the judge to get situated.

Judge Mathers shifted stacks of files from one side of the bench to the other, flipping through them while moving them around. He finally yanked a folder from a stack of case files and set it in front of him.

The judge had thinned gray hair and a scholarly air about him. He had been on the bench for a couple decades. Prior to becoming a judge, he'd served as a prosecutor. He wore spectacles with silver, wire frames. Judge Mathers had led a fairly academic life in the law with a meager salary. One could easily picture him as a history or English professor.

After he was settled, the judge perused the lawyers. "Please identify yourselves for the record," he said in a perfunctory tone.

"John Marshall, for the Commonwealth, Your Honor," the D.A. said.

"Nice to see you, Mr. District Attorney," the judge said kindly.

"Jared Wheeler for the Commonwealth as well."

"Nice to meet you," said Judge Mathers.

"Kenneth Dwyer for the defendant, Trevor Belliveau."

"Yes, Mr. Dwyer," the judge said derisively. "I see you've moved to the other side of the aisle."

Ken got the feeling the judge had taken offense to a fine young prosecutor moving over to the defense. Judge Mathers probably felt that a person with Ken's background should stick with civil service positions. The move was likely seen as a pursuit of money. Rather, Ken felt it was a pursuit of freedom.

The freedom that comes from running your own business.

"What are we here for?" Judge Matters said, looking from one counsel table to the other. "A motion to suppress?"

"Yes, Your Honor," all the lawyers replied in unison.

"Mr. Dwyer, it's your motion," the judge said. "You can begin."

Ken straightened his materials, then he marched to the podium located between the two tables. The prosecutors sat down.

After straightening his papers, Ken looked up and met the expectant eyes of the judge.

"Your Honor, this motion to suppress is twofold," Ken said. "First, the search was undertaken without a warrant. There weren't any exigent circumstances. Officers undertook the search in the defendant's dedicated space. He had a lease and occupied a portion of the basement. The property owner had no right to consent to a search of her tenant's property."

"Wasn't the property owner a relative?" the judge asked.

"That has no bearing on this issue," Ken retorted.

"Your pleadings are well-briefed," Judge Mathers said. "Better than most found in cases like this, filed by criminal defense lawyers. The affidavit, photographs, and argument are well developed. Do you have anything else on this issue?"

The judge was trying to cut the oral argument short.

Ken took a deep breath. "Secondly, the search did not result in the seizure of contraband. The police confiscated tools the defendant uses in his business..."

Judge Mathers frowned. "Do you have anything else to add? I'd really like to hear from the Commonwealth on these points."

"If you feel the briefing is sound, then I will allow the Commonwealth to speak now. However, I request an opportunity for follow up."

"You may have it, if necessary." Judge Mathers looked at opposing counsel. "Mr. District Attorney, you may proceed."

Marshall stood up as Ken left the podium.

Stepping to the podium, Marshall carried a notepad with a

few comments jotted on the first page. He set it down and smiled like a politician. "We'd like to address the second point first, Your Honor."

"You may," Judge Mathers said kindly.

"We have a Boston police officer here, who we'd like to call as a witness," Marshall said, pointing to an officer seated in the gallery. "He was a member of the task force."

"Go ahead," the judge said.

"Officer O'Rourke, please take the stand," Marshall said.

The officer stood up. He was young with short black hair, and his uniform appeared to be tailor fitted to his lean, muscular body. O'Rourke walked confidently across the well of the courtroom to the witness box.

He stood patiently and was sworn in. Then, he sat down comfortably, like he'd done numerous times.

Marshall started to walk the officer through his investigation.

"We had a C.I.," O'Rourke said. "A confidential informant."

"Hold up," the judge said. "I don't want to get us too afoul of the purpose of this hearing. As the Supreme Judicial Court said in *Commonwealth v. Roy*, a motion to suppress hearing should be limited to the items seized and the manner in which they were seized. It should not be used as an opportunity for free discovery into the police investigation by the defense."

Ken stood. "Your Honor, this question wasn't asked by the defense."

"The principal remains true," Judge Mathers chided him.

"I'll rephrase," Marshall said.

Ken sat down.

"Officer O'Rourke, what did you seize?" Marshall said.

"We found pry bars of various sizes, a drill, drill bits, cutting tools, and a heavy-duty mallet," O'Rourke said.

"Do you have any experience investigating burglaries?"

"Yes," O'Rourke said. "I'm not a detective, but I respond to and investigate burglaries all the time, including homes, businesses and pharmacies."

"What type of items are used for commercial break-ins?"

"The type of items we seized from the defendant. Pry bars, cutting tools, drills, and mallets."

Judge Mathers grinned proudly at the response.

Marshall continued, "And you had information the defendant was involved in—"

"Objection!" Ken bellowed, rising to his feet.

"Basis?" the judge asked.

"Foundation."

"Sustained."

"Your Honor," Marshall pled. "You're tying my hands here."

The judge waved the comment off. "The objection is sustained. Please continue."

"How did you come to seize the burglary tools from the defendant?"

"We had reason to believe the defendant was involved in..."

Ken stood. "This is—"

"Overruled," Judge Mathers said. "This is just merely foundation as to the reason for the search. Previously, the prosecution sought to introduce the testimony as a basis for the crime that was charged. At that point, it did not have foundation and it served as a conclusion. This is entirely different. Please proceed."

"Like I was saying," O'Rourke continued. "We had reason to believe the defendant was involved in a string of pharmacy break-ins. This caused us to visit the house."

"What happened when you got there?"

O'Rourke shrugged, like everything he had to say from here was an innocent turn of events. "We went to the house to interview the defendant. Get his side of the story."

"And what happened?"

"He wasn't home."

"And then?"

"Then his aunt came out and asked if she could help us."

"What did you do?"

"I asked her if we could look around the house."

"What did she do?"

"She told us we could." O'Rourke smiled like something was funny. "Then she proceeded to lead us around the house, showing us everything. Letting us look around."

"And where did that lead?"

"It led us to a storage locker in the basement. We anticipated the defendant had burglary tools in the house. And we found them in the storage locker."

"What did you do from there?"

"We bagged them and tagged them as evidence. Then we charged the defendant with conspiracy to commit burglary. He turned himself in."

Marshall cracked a broad grin. "Your Honor, that's all I have for now."

"Mr. Dwyer, any cross?" asked the judge.

Ken stood and moved into the well of the courtroom to confront the witness. "The items that you confiscated can be used in a construction business, right?"

"Sure. They can be used for break-ins, too." O'Rourke chuckled.

"You haven't tied the tools you confiscated with any crime that you're investigating?"

"Not at this time," O'Rourke admitted. "We see them as being used for a future crime."

"You saw boxes located on the carpet near the storage locker?"

"O'Rourke looked confused, like he didn't know where this was going. "Yeah. There were some boxes down there," he said sarcastically. "It was a basement."

A few people in the gallery laughed. O'Rourke flashed a proud grin.

"You didn't open any to see that the defendant actually ran a construction business?"

"No." O'Rourke sounded befuddled.

"There was nothing illegal about the tools confiscated?"

"Sir?" O'Rourke said. "I'm afraid that I don't quite follow."

"The tools you confiscated weren't contraband?" asked Ken. "Right?"

"No. They were not contraband."

"The tools you seized weren't illegal to own."

"No. They weren't illegal, in and of themselves."

"Running a construction business is a good reason to own tools?"

"Sure. And running a break-in gang is, too."

"You didn't get a warrant?"

"No. Like I was—"

Ken stepped closer and held up his hand. "Thank you, officer. You answered my question."

O'Rourke sat in the witness box, looking dumbfounded.

"You searched the unit upstairs."

"Yes."

"The defendant lived in that unit alone, right?"

O'Rourke nodded, then said reluctantly, "Yes. That's true."

"You found boxes and exercise equipment on an area of carpet near the back of the basement, right?"

"We did see that stuff there, but…"

Ken held up his hand and O'Rourke stopped talking. "May I approach, Your Honor."

"You may," said Judge Mathers.

Ken walked over to his counsel table and grabbed a copy of his motion. Then, he flipped to the photographs of the basement, as he walked towards the witness stand.

Standing alongside the witness, Ken said, "Are those fair and accurate pictures of the basement?"

"Yes," O'Rourke said. "But that ain't how those boxes looked."

"Are you saying this picture doesn't reflect the conditions found on the day of the search?"

"That's exactly what I'm sayin'," O'Rourke replied. "The aunt's boxes were mixed in with the defendant's boxes."

"How can we trust your memory?"

"We took pictures of the cellar," O'Rourke boasted.

"Can you tell me where the police photographs are located?"

"Right there," O'Rourke said, pointing to the prosecutors' table.

Ken spun around and walked to the prosecution table.

Marshall handed over the photographs, and Ken flipped through them as he returned to the center of the courtroom.

Judge Mathers perked up. "I just want to be sure those are just photographs of the premises that is the subject of this motion."

"They are, Your Honor," Marshall said.

Ken approached the witness and showed him a single photograph. "Is this a fair and accurate picture of the storage locker prior to your seizing the tools."

"It is," O'Rourke said, proudly.

Ken showed the photograph to the judge, then he walked over and showed it to Marshall. Both of them nodded when they had seen enough of it.

Returning to the witness, Ken said, "This locker only contained the defendant's tools?"

"Yup."

"Nothing else?"

"Nope."

"You didn't find any of the aunt's possessions in there, right?"

O'Rourke looked like a deer in headlights. "Ahh, no," he muttered.

Ken pulled out another photograph taken by the police. "Please tell us if this is a fair and accurate picture you took of the front of the storage locker in question."

"It is," O'Rourke said, sounding sullen.

Ken showed the photograph to the judge, then walked over and showed it to Marshall. A full gallery in the courtroom, and Ken could feel the tension rising at the prosecution table. Marshall looked worried.

Ken returned to the witness. "Please read what is written on the masking tape on the front of the locker door."

"Trevor Belliveau."

"And that tape looks old and worn?"

"Yes."

"It was there at the time of your search?"

"Yes." O'Rourke shrugged.

"The storage locker and all its contents belonged to a tenant of the property, right?"

"Apparently so," O'Rourke mumbled.

ELEVEN

RETURNING to his table, Ken stood and waited to see how the prosecution would respond.

The judge looked at Marshall. "Anything further?"

Marshall shook his head. He clearly knew when to let it go. "No, Your Honor."

"Well then," Judge Mathers said. "The motion to suppress is denied."

Ken couldn't believe what he just heard. "Your Honor?" he protested.

Judge Mathers held up a hand. "Just hold on."

"But, Your Honor," Ken pressed. "They seized—"

"Enough!" Judge Mathers shouted. Then, he took a moment to gather himself.

Ken waited, wondering what the judge planned to do.

"The motion is denied," Judge Mathers continued. "However, I am dismissing this case without prejudice to refile at a later date. The police shall retain custody of the tools through the winter. If new charges are not filed by April 1st next year, the tools shall be returned to the defendant."

Marshall nodded. He probably thought that was the best result the police and prosecution could expect under the circumstances.

Ken realized the ruling was likely meant to stave off a civil lawsuit. "The defense asks that you reconsider," Ken said.

"You have my ruling," the judge replied. "We'll get a written decision issued this afternoon. Anything else?"

"No, Your Honor," Marshall said.

Ken shook his head, dismayed. "No, sir."

"You may be excused," Judge Mathers said.

As counsel packed up their bags, the judge addressed the gallery. "The court shall take a five-minute recess."

He whisked off the bench, headed to a door in the back of the courtroom. His robe dragged on the floor behind him. Then the sessions clerk rose from his table and instructed the gallery to return promptly and to remember to turn their cellphones off when they came back.

Turning to the pews, Ken approached his client. Belliveau had a broad grin and looked entirely amused by the ordeal.

"Nice going," Belliveau said.

Ken didn't care for the possibility of the charge being reinstated. The matter would hang over his client's head. But he was also pissed at Belliveau.

"We need to talk outside," Ken said, grabbing his overcoat. Then, he stormed for the door.

TWELVE

EXITING the courtroom, Ken couldn't get through the throng of people leaving for the five-minute break. Several attorneys applauded him on his performance. He just nodded, completely disinterested in the praise. Ken had a bigger fish to fry.

He ran into more resistance on the landing outside the courtroom doors. Lawyers and clients were chatting about their matters. A few attorneys had pulled out their flip phones and were ambling about trying to get reception.

Ken finally plied his way past the crowd. Belliveau trailed a few feet behind him.

Ken found an unoccupied attorney/client meeting room and stepped inside.

When Belliveau closed the door, Ken stepped close and stood face-to-face with the young man. "You've got some nerve," Ken snapped.

"Did I miss something?" Belliveau said. "I thought we won in there."

"You haven't been straight with me," Ken barked. "I saw their photographs. You moved the boxes around."

Belliveau stared at him, looking sad. "It's not what you think."

"Tell me what I think?" Ken insisted.

"You think that all my stuff and my aunt's stuff were piled in the basement together," Belliveau said. "And you think that I sorted it out before you got there. Making it look like we had two separate areas."

"Isn't that what happened?" asked Ken.

"No," Belliveau said, shaking his head. "It wasn't like that at all."

"What was it, then?" Ken said.

Belliveau stepped past Ken and took a seat at the table. "I'll tell you. But you need to calm down and listen."

Ken draped his coat over the back of the chair and sat down across from his client.

"We always kept our stuff separate," Belliveau explained. "She had most of the cellar and I had the area that I showed you. And the storage locker was mine, just like you thought."

"So, what's with the boxes?"

"It was *them*," Belliveau said, clearly meaning the police.

"Explain."

"After we started talking on the phone about dedicated space," Belliveau said. "I went down there to take a look. I was mostly planning to look for the lease. I remembered that I had to have one to register my car. Anyway... I found boxes of my aunt's stuff had been moved over to my area. The police had done it. I just moved them back. Honest."

"How do you know it wasn't your aunt?"

Belliveau shook his head. "No way."

"Why not?"

"For one thing, she's quite old. And another is that she doesn't go down there."

"Maybe she did?" Ken said.

"Nope," Belliveau said. "Whenever she wants something, she asks me to go down there and get it for her. Decorations for the holidays. Stuff like that. It's an old house with steep stairs. She wouldn't risk it."

Ken sat back and mulled it over. Everything the kid had explained made sense.

"Sorry if I wasn't completely straight with you," Belliveau said, apologetically. "Just I didn't want to risk going to prison because some fucking cop didn't play it straight to begin with. Besides, you knocked the case out without relying upon what I did."

The explanation eased Ken's feelings about the situation. He hadn't relied upon the overall dedicated space in the basement to get the case kicked. But he had relied upon photographs in his motion. Then he considered the affidavit used in support of the motion. Belliveau had insisted on stating that the photographs represented the condition of the property prior to the search.

Belliveau was smarter than he initially had thought. Maybe too smart.

"Listen," Ken said after a moment. "You need to always be straight with your lawyer. That stunt could have blown up on us. And you'd be spending the night in a cell."

"Understood."

"A lawyer needs to know the downside facts in order to work around them. If I'd known about the boxes being moved, I might have thought of isolating the storage locker sooner. Instead, I came up with it on my feet on the fly, and you're lucky it went down that way."

"Agreed." Belliveau flashed a smile. "Are we good?"

"I guess so," Ken said, standing. "For now. Come on, let's get out of here."

THIRTEEN

LEAVING the courthouse, Ken and Belliveau ran into Marshall on the sidewalk. He was talking on a flip phone, and someone was yelling on the other end of the call.

"Tell Dan that I said hello," Ken called to Marshall.

Marshall grinned and nodded. "Ken Dwyer pays his respects," Marshall said into the phone, looking amused.

More shouting ensued. Marshall looked at Ken and shrugged.

Clearly, Dan Collins had called in a favor and asked Marshall to handle this hearing personally. Marshall had probably agreed to do so and stuck his neck out on a flimsy case. Collins probably hadn't filled him in on all the details. The Suffolk County District Attorney probably hadn't informed his Essex County counterpart that he was just using Marshall to help get a result to avoid a civil lawsuit. The investigation was likely a multi-jurisdiction task force with the Suffolk County District Attorney's Office spearheading the entire operation.

After Collins blew up over the result, Marshall seemed to take a perverse pleasure in passing along the greeting. Lawyers had huge egos.

Considering the magnitude of the investigation, the matter probably went high up and could implicate the tactics of some very politically astute adversaries. The issue of prescription drug addiction was hot in the press and Collins was likely looking for a big arrest to make a splash in the news. Ken wondered how far the police and prosecution would go to protect themselves.

He also wondered what kind of trouble Belliveau was mixed

up with.

FOURTEEN

WALKING down the sidewalk, Ken felt a release from the pressure of having the hearing behind him. He headed towards the parking garage down the street from the courthouse, and Belliveau dawdled along beside him.

The kid was recounting the exciting moments from the hearing. Ken just wanted to get back to the office and catch up on some pleadings that he needed to get filed.

"You parked in the garage?" Ken asked, wondering if the kid would accompany him there.

"No," Belliveau said. "I've got a spot on the street back that way."

Belliveau stopped and pointed. Ken halted and traced where the kid had indicated. The black Chevy was parked at a meter, and it was a block behind them.

"Aren't you concerned about getting a ticket," Ken said. "We were inside long enough for the two-hour limit to have expired."

Belliveau shook his head and chuckled. "Nope."

"Why not?" Ken wondered if Belliveau had a friend in the Salem police.

"I just toss them in the trash," Belliveau said with a shrug.

Ken considered the comment. This guy was a risk taker and could only lead to trouble.

"Well, I've got to get back to the office," Ken said, hoping Belliveau would get the point.

"That's okay," Belliveau said. "I can walk you to your car."

"Listen, that's not necessary," Ken said, starting down the sidewalk.

Belliveau hesitated. As Ken began to spread the distance between them, the kid trotted over and caught up to him.

"I was thinking... we should talk about the civil case," Belliveau said.

Ken was thinking about dropping that matter altogether. This might be a suitable time to disincentivize him. "Sure. Let's grab a coffee."

"I know a place right around the corner," Belliveau said.

"Lead the way," Ken said, wondering if this meeting was a mistake.

A colleague who had hung out a shingle once told Ken to avoid social settings with individual clients because it could lead to problems. Ken was working as a prosecutor and had already experienced certain pressures from police officers after getting to know them on a personal level.

They walked down a pristine sidewalk and the kid stopped in front of a brick building with large plate-glass windows.

"Here we are," Belliveau said.

Ken glanced inside. "This doesn't look like a coffee shop."

"You can order a coffee. I'm starvin' and need something to eat."

Entering the upscale restaurant and bar, Ken felt a sinking feeling and wondered where this would lead. He wasn't sure it would be easy to drop this client.

The place had a large bar with metal barstools, plank floors, exposed brick walls, and an unfinished ceiling with exposed pipes. Incandescent lightbulbs hung from the ceiling and the woodwork had a brushed feel, like broken-in tee shirts. The floor space was packed with high-top tables, and flatscreen televisions hung on the walls. It reminded Ken of bars in Lexington, Memphis, and Nashville where he'd frequented during his Army days.

At mid-afternoon, the place was completely dead. They sat down at a spot with a jog in the bar, which was further away from the tables in the dining area.

Ken glanced around for a menu, but the bar top was spotless.

A few minutes later, a stout younger man with a bushy beard pushed through a swinging door from out back. He stepped behind the bar and approached them.

"I'm Zack," he said, flashing a friendly smile.

He wore blue jeans, a tee shirt with the bar's logo on the breast pocket. He also had a black baseball cap that sported the logo. Reaching under the counter, he grabbed a dish rag and wiped the counter down. It was spotless, but he did it anyway.

"You guys planning to stay with us for a bit?" Zack asked.

"I could go for a coffee," Ken said.

Zack looked disappointed. Then he turned to Belliveau. "And you?"

"I'd like to take a look at the menu," Belliveau said.

"Sure thing," Zack replied, sounding happy again.

Reaching under the bar, Zack pulled out a menu and placed it in front of Belliveau. He placed a craft beer list on top of it. Ken wondered how long this little coffee break would end up cutting into his day.

"Thanks," Belliveau said.

"I'll be right back with the coffee," Zack said.

"Can I get a glass of water," Belliveau said, calling after him.

"Sure thing."

When Zack was gone, Belliveau added, "I'm parched."

It was another odd comment that made Ken wonder about the guy. Belliveau was a kid from a working-class town, who probably just barely graduated from the local vocational high school. The kid seemed to want to impress Ken with language that nobody even used in the suburbs where Ken had grown up.

Ken wanted to dive into strategic discussion about the civil case, but Belliveau had his nose in the menu and seemed to be engrossed with the selections.

Eventually, Zack returned and placed a glass of water and a cup of coffee down. "Decide what you want yet?"

"I'll take the Derby burger with fries on the side," Belliveau said.

"Anything to drink?"

"Sure. I'll go with your IPA."

Zack grinned. "You'll love it. Our most popular brew."

After Zack left, Ken dove into the civil case. "This was a good result," he said. "But it was designed to make you reconsider filing a civil case."

"How so?" Belliveau replied, looking at him skeptically.

"The judge left the matter open. They could file new charges anytime."

Belliveau shook his head. "If they could bring serious charges, they would have done so already. Besides, they would have gotten a warrant if they had anything concrete."

His remarks were accurate. They also did not protest innocence.

"Your criminal charges could just go away. That's all I'm saying."

"I'm not willing to drop the civil matter," Belliveau said.

"Suit yourself," Ken said. "But you've been advised of the risks."

"Duly noted."

Zack returned and placed a pint of beer down. "Your order should be ready in just a bit. Can I get you anything else?"

"I'm all set," Belliveau grumbled.

Zack looked at him, wondering if he'd done something to upset the man.

"Thanks," Ken said, kindly. "I'm good."

Zack left and Ken took a sip of coffee. Belliveau had suddenly turned melancholy and Ken didn't have any idea what had put the morse behavior into motion.

Belliveau took a sip of his beer, then looked up at a television hanging on the wall behind the bar. A sports talk show was on, and the kid seemed entirely disinterested. He slid the menus to the side, then fished his cellphone out of his suit pocket and started checking messages.

He doesn't like sports, Ken thought.

A few minutes later, Zack returned with a plate loaded with the burger and fries. He set it down in front of Belliveau.

Belliveau beamed. "That looks great."

"Are you guys all set?" asked Zack.

"Sure," Belliveau replied. "We know where to find you, buddy."

Ken took another sip of his coffee. He considered whether he should just have ordered a burger. He was going to have to wait through Belliveau's meal anyway. The burger looked good, with a buttered roll and a thick patty.

"It's not too late to get you one," Zack offered.

Belliveau took a bite of his burger. "This is fantastic. Ken, you should really get one."

"Okay, what the heck," Ken said.

Zack grinned. "Coming right up. Do you want to switch up your beverage?"

"Sure." Ken laughed. "I'll go with a glass of Buffalo Trace and a water."

"Best bourbon on the menu for a burger like that," Zack said. "I'll be right back."

Ken told Belliveau that he was going to use the restroom.

When he returned, Ken found a burger and fries set next to his cellphone, and the drinks he ordered were situated to the side of the plate.

Soon, they were both digging into their meals and already on a second round of drinks. Belliveau made several sarcastic jokes, which were misplaced with Ken as an audience. But the humor was meant to be lighthearted, and Ken wondered if he'd judged the kid too harshly. The conversation had slipped into a lull as they polished off their meals.

"I might have another matter for you to handle," Belliveau said, breaking the silence.

"Shoot," Ken said. The drinks had gone to his head, and he was feeling relaxed.

"Funny that you say that," Belliveau replied.

"Why?"

"The matter involves firearms."

"There are lawyers that specialize in firearms," Ken said.

"Sure. But it's not a firearms case per se."

"What's it about?"

"I've told you that I'm going through a divorce…"

"We don't handle any family law matters."

Belliveau tossed what was left of his burger on the plate. "Will you just let me get this out?" he snapped.

"Go ahead," Ken said.

"I've had a side business, where I do some gunsmithing," Belliveau said, gesticulating. "During the divorce proceeding, my wife got a restraining order."

"Is it still in effect?"

"No," Belliveau said, shaking his head. "It ran out a year ago. But during the time it was in place, the judge ordered that I sell all my firearms."

"I'm no divorce lawyer, but I understand that's fairly standard."

"Sure. But the firearms were turned over to this dealer and he's misreporting the value of various items. I'm supposed to get half of the sales price, less their commission. They report sales way below market value."

"What's in it for them?"

"I can think of several reasons."

Ken thought about it. He could see a shady gun dealer trying to take advantage of a divorce matter. They could easily gin up a set of books to reflect the sales prices they reported.

Belliveau took a swig of his beer. "So—"

Ken's phone buzzed. He held up his hand for Belliveau to hold on.

Reaching into a suit coat pocket, Ken fished out his phone and saw that Mickey was checking in on him. Ken slid off his bar stool and walked towards the far side of the restaurant. He accepted the call, "Ken Dwyer here."

"Ken, glad that I caught you," Mickey said.

"What's up?"

"I heard about the great result today."

"How did you learn about it so fast?" Ken asked.

"Listen, I've got little birds that land on my shoulders and tell me things."

"So, you just called to congratulate me?" Ken questioned Mickey's intentions.

"That... and I'm wondering if you're having second thoughts about the civil case."

"He wants to go forward with it, despite the risk."

"You told him about the risks?"

"Sure. Why do you ask?"

"Make certain to write a memo on a notepad about that discussion. Might come in handy if he gets arrested again."

"Okay," Ken said. "He wants us to take on another matter."

"About what?"

"Something to do with a gun dealer selling his firearms at below market prices."

"Take it!" Mickey bellowed.

"You sure?"

"Definitely," Mickey replied. "Make sure to get a five grand retainer for the firearms case and three thousand for an expense retainer in the police misconduct matter."

"Okay, I'll ask."

"Don't ask. Insist."

"All right."

"Ken, you have to strike while the moment is hot. You just got a fantastic result. Now, the client wants you to take on more cases. Push like a real lawyer, like what a lawyer in demand would require... and demand the retainers to continue representation."

"Got it. Anything else?"

"Nope. That's it."

Ken ended the call and headed back over to the bar. He climbed onto his stool and took a long sip of his bourbon.

Belliveau stared at him with a guileful look on his face.

"Listen," Ken said. "That was Mickey. He needs you to pay a couple retainers."

"No problem," Belliveau said.

Ken explained the terms. Then, he polished off his glass.

Pulling out his wallet, Ken said, "Ready to go."

"Sure."

They settled the tab with Zack, then headed for the door.

Stepping outside, Ken felt dizzy, and the sidewalk seemed slanted, like he was about to drop off into the street. His head suddenly buzzed. Everything looked blurry.

FIFTEEN

KEN felt a cool breeze wash over him, as the car whisked along Route 1 north of Boston. He was disoriented and unsure of events since leaving the bar. It was a pitch-black night. Neon signs lit up the roadside, making everything appear surreal.

Where did the afternoon go? Ken thought.

Music blared on the car stereo. Something heavy and unfamiliar.

"There you are," said a voice from the driver's seat.

Ken was a passenger in his own car. He couldn't piece things together; everything was disjointed. It was like being concussed on the battlefield after a mortar attack.

Things appeared in slow motion, as the car zipped past liquor outlets, chain restaurants, and adult entertainment stores.

"Was beginning to think I'd lost you," Belliveau said, chuckling.

"Huh?" Ken didn't follow.

"You've had yourself quite a night."

Ken didn't understand. *How could it be nighttime?*

"To tell you the truth," Belliveau said. "I'd thought you were a bit of a stiff."

"What?" Ken stammered.

"Boy did you prove me wrong."

"Huh?"

"Whoa!"

"Ah?"

"This night is going down in the books," Belliveau said,

laughing.

Ken tried to piece things together, but he kept coming up blank. It was literally just blackness that came to mind. What he could recall was foggy. Unclear.

Belliveau's comments and sadistic laughter had him on edge. Ken wondered what had gone down. Glancing out the window, the neon lights hurt his eyes. He squinted and his head hurt, like a chisel was being driven into his skull.

Flashes of neon lighting came to mind. Not neon lights, but strobe lights.

Darkness and strobe lights. Flesh.

Ken recalled nude dancers on a stage. Pole dancers.

"What the hell?" Ken muttered. *Was it a dream?*

"Some of it's starting to come back?" Belliveau said.

Ken nodded. "Where have we been?"

"Don't worry about it."

Belliveau braked and whipped the car off the roadway.

They rolled up to a dilapidated parking lot of a roadside all-night coffee shop.

Belliveau shifted into park. "I'll be back in a minute."

Ken watched the thug ordering at a window. Belliveau leaned on a ledge while he waited for the order. A server slid a window open and shoved something through; two cups of coffee. Everything he observed was blurry, and his stomach felt queasy.

Belliveau moved over to a condiments stand, located further down on the shelf.

A minute later, Belliveau returned with a couple of coffees.

"You need one of these to clear your mind," Belliveau said, handing over a coffee.

Ken grabbed the cup and took a sip. "This is awful."

"What do you mean?" Belliveau said, downing his coffee quickly.

"It's loaded with cream and sugar."

"Makes it taste better and cools it off," Belliveau said.

"Here, take it," Ken said, trying to hand it over.

"I'm not taking that. You've got to drink it."

Belliveau shifted into reverse. He backed the car around, then he gunned it out of the parking lot, tearing back onto Route 1.

Ken took a couple more sips of the coffee. It was lukewarm and tasted like sugary milk.

He figured it might help settle his stomach, so he took a long swig.

You've got to drink it. Ken recalled the comment with alarm.

Ken dumped the rest of the coffee out the window and shoved the cup into a compartment in the console. Then he curled up against the door and passed out.

SIXTEEN

NEXT morning, Ken awoke to the sound of someone rapping on a car window. He slowly came around and managed to focus his eyes. He was slumped in the front passenger seat of his car.

Mickey stood outside of the car with a confused look on his face.

Somehow, the Volkswagen was parked in the small lot behind the office.

The car was basic and old enough to have window cranks, so Ken rolled down the window. He wanted to cry out and ask how he'd gotten there. "What's going on?" Ken said. It was all he could manage to say.

"That's what I was going to ask you," Mickey said.

Ken tried to think back. The night was blurred in his mind. His last memory was walking out of the bar in Salem. Then he recalled a stop at a roadside coffee shop.

"I don't know," Ken said with a shrug.

"Well, if you don't know, then I certainly don't," Mickey said, cracking a smile.

"Sorry," Ken said. But he wasn't sure what he was apologetic about.

"That's okay," Mickey said. "Happens to the best of us."

Ken fumbled around trying to find his car keys. They were seated in the cupholder in the center console. The coffee cups were gone.

Mickey opened the door for him. "Come on, get out of there."

Ken grabbed the overhead handle and managed to roll out of the car and get to his feet.

He teetered for a moment, and Mickey grabbed him, trying to provide stability.

"Boy, you really tied one on last night," Mickey said.

Ken smiled, but he wasn't even sure if that was the case. He didn't remember ordering more than a couple drinks. He took a deep breath. "I've got it," he said. Then, he ambled down the alleyway headed towards State Street.

Mickey walked alongside him. "You know that you're not supposed to park there."

"Yup. Just let me get settled and I'll move it in a bit."

"No time," Mickey said. "You have to defend a deposition upstairs, starting in an hour. I'll call the landlord and straighten it out."

"Deposition?" Ken said, surprised.

SEVENTEEN

KEN went into his office and found a bag of ablutions in the bottom drawer of his desk. Then he headed to the bathroom to shave and brush his teeth.

Glancing into the mirror, he looked awful. A ghastly person stared back at him, with unkempt hair, dark circles under his eyes and a sallow complexion. He looked like someone with health issues, or worse, a guy struggling with substance abuse.

He splashed water on his face, then ran some water through his hair and combed it.

Ken cleaned up and felt a little better. Then he headed back towards his office and ran into Pat in front of the elevators.

"Good morning," he said.

"Morning to you," she said, skeptically.

He kept walking, hoping she didn't think he had been out drinking all night. But he suspected that was exactly what she had been thinking.

Once in his office, Ken stored the toiletry bag away and hunted down a tie.

Ken struggled to get the tie on without use of a mirror. As soon as he was satisfied that it was cinched properly, his phone rang. He looked at the caller ID and saw that Pat was calling him.

He reached for the receiver, "Hello?"

"Your client is here," Pat said, with a hint of amusement in her voice.

Ken hadn't a moment to settle in and he was already back putting on a live performance. His head ached and he needed some pain relief.

Stepping out of his office, Ken leaned over and whispered to Pat, "Can you get me two aspirin and a cup of water?"

"Sure," Pat said, standing up.

"Pull me out of the conference room saying that I have a call once you've got everything together," he added. "I'll take them out here."

"Understood." Pat flashed a mischievous grin.

Ken walked down the corridor and met a middle-aged woman seated in a reception chair.

"Hello, I'm Ken Dwyer," he said, cheerfully. "Let's step into the conference room."

PART THREE

POLICE MISCONDUCT CASE

EIGHTEEN

KEN sat in the conference room, defending the deposition of a trip and fall client he had only met briefly that morning.

The fall had occurred at a step in the outside common area of a condominium complex. A couple of theories had been presented in the lawsuit, including the edge of the step needing to be painted yellow, and the step being an inch higher than allowed by the building code.

It was a multi-party case with several defendants, and lawyers were packed into the tight space. Ken had sat through a lot of mundane questioning from the insurance defense attorney who had noticed the deposition.

The questioning hadn't gone anywhere and the lawyer's attempts to place the fault of the incident on the plaintiff had gone over like a lead balloon.

A younger lawyer representing a different defendant took over questioning the plaintiff.

This lawyer was sharp and well prepared. He began questioning the witness about the trivial details of her activities. He asked her whether she had encountered the step at the end of the walkway before. It turns out that she used the walkway on a regular basis to fetch her mail. The plaintiff had actually traversed the step fifteen minutes prior to the incident.

These facts could result in the case taking a drastic turn.

Ken sat up straight and began objecting to questions in order to break up the momentum the young lawyer had gained.

There was a knock on the conference room door.

Pat stuck her head into the room. "You have an emergency

call," she said to Ken.

"Let's take a five-minute break," Ken said to the lawyers.

He walked out of the room and headed down the hall to his office.

Stepping inside, the phone was already ringing from Pat putting the caller through. He shut the door and reached for the receiver.

"Ken Dwyer," he said.

"Hey, Ken," Belliveau said. "How are we coming with the lawsuit?"

"The lawsuit?"

"Yeah. You were planning to draft the civil lawsuit."

Ken couldn't believe what he was hearing. "We discussed that yesterday."

"Sure," Belliveau said. "Figured you'd gotten started on it this morning. I hadn't seen anything, so I thought that I'd check in."

"Listen," Ken snapped. "Lawyers don't just handle one case. Did it ever cross your mind that I was already booked for this morning?"

Belliveau didn't respond.

"A lawsuit like this takes time to draft in order to get it right. This isn't something that can be ginned up in a morning."

"Okay," Belliveau said, backing down. But he sounded peeved.

"I've got to go. You interrupted a deposition."

"How long will it take?"

"About a week," Ken said. "However, you need to account for emergencies in my schedule and responding to unanticipated motions that get filed by other counsel, which require a quick response. We can't always plan our days in this business."

"Sure, you're a busy guy," Belliveau said. "I get it."

"I'll be in touch next week. And do me a favor..."

"What?"

"Please don't call the office looking for me, saying that something is an emergency... when it clearly isn't."

Belliveau huffed. "Okay, sure."

Ken hung up the phone. Then he stepped into the hallway and walked over to Pat's desk. She looked up at him, expectantly.

"That guy isn't to interrupt me for any reason," Ken said.

"Understood." Pat grinned. Then, she looked back down at her work.

Ken returned to the conference room, figuring the trip and fall case would come down to the code issue and the claim against the engineer who had designed the step and walkway.

Easing back into his chair, Ken wondered about Belliveau. The guy didn't seem to be employed and had nothing but time on his hands. Belliveau was going to make a hobby of his legal matters. Ken had seen it before.

And Belliveau was going to live rent free in Ken's head, too.

NINETEEN

A GRAY afternoon sky had turned to nighttime, and Ken watched snow flurries whisk past the conference room window.

The deposition of the slip and fall plaintiff had taken an entire day. It could have been handled in a few hours, but each defense lawyer felt the need to ask his own questions, often repeating the areas covered by other attorneys.

At times, the defense lawyers had reported they were almost through. This led to everyone working through lunch.

Now, it was evening, and the streetlights were lit up outside. Lights in the offices across the street were slowly shutting off, one by one, eventually the building looked empty and dark.

When the defense lawyers had finally finished questioning the witness, they packed up their black trial bags with documents. Ken led them out to the reception area, where they slid into their overcoats then shuffled into the lift.

Once the elevator doors rattled shut, Ken went to the conference room to debrief with his client. The stenographer was packing up her equipment, so he stood by the bookcase while he waited for her. She finally got her things shoved into a rollaboard and hustled out of the conference room, saying goodbye to Ken on her way out.

Ken told his client that she had done a fantastic job and the deposition had not done anything to get the case entirely dismissed. He explained some unfortunate developments, but he provided her with encouragement about the building code issue. She had also done well at explaining complications from her fractured ankle.

Then he escorted her to the elevator and waited until she was inside.

When the elevator doors closed, he turned around and found the reception area empty. The place was silent. He walked to the back of the suite, checking offices and cubicles. Everyone had gone home.

Ken headed to his office and reviewed his emails.

He felt a buzz in his suit jacket pocket. Fishing out his flip phone, Ken opened it.

He had received a text message from Alyson: *Dinner?*

His stomach churned from skipping lunch. Ken couldn't decide what he craved more, a shower or a meal.

The whole texting craze had just begun, and Ken wasn't really adept at it. He couldn't figure out what keys to press and it often took longer than just making a short call. His phone had the ability to save several contacts and Alyson was at the top of the list. Ken decided to call her, rather than play around at texting back and forth.

He pressed a button and heard a dial tone.

"This is Alyson," she said.

"Figured it might be easier to just have a short call."

"You really do need to learn how to text."

"Afraid I'm a bit cumbersome at it."

"They have new phones coming out that will make it easier," she offered.

Ken thought about the cellphone Belliveau used and wondered how an unemployed young man could afford such a device. "Someday I'll get one," Ken said after a moment.

"Are you up for dinner?" she asked.

"Sure. But I can't do it downtown."

"Why not?"

"I've got to get home and take a shower."

"A shower?"

"Yeah. It's a long story."

"Sure. *Okay.*"

"We can talk about it at dinner," Ken said. "Do you just want to meet me at a restaurant in Brighton?"

There was a pause, like she was mulling it over.

"Listen," Ken said. "If you don't want to get together tonight..."

"No, I want to get together tonight," she replied. "I've got some news."

"Okay. Let's hit Article Twenty-Four."

"All right." She sounded glum.

"What's wrong?"

"This is good news," Alyson said. "I kind of wanted to have a mini celebration. You know, in *town*."

"If that's what you want, we can do it. But Article Twenty-Four has a trendy atmosphere."

Another pause. "We'll do that. It will be different."

"Sounds great. Does an hour work for you?"

"Let's make it an hour and a half. I've got a few things to catch up on."

"See you there," Ken said, ending the call.

He shut down his computer and turned off the lights. Then, he headed down in the lift and stepped into a blustery night. Winds howled down State Street. Snowflakes cascaded from the darkness above and whisked around in a frenzy.

Ken decided to leave his car in the lot behind the building. He ducked his head down and trundled up the sidewalk towards the public transit line.

Somehow, he felt like he was being watched.

Peering over his shoulder, Ken scanned the recesses and crannies of the building across the street, where limestone jutted from the façade. The spaces were dark, and he couldn't spot anyone loitering in the shadows.

Just as he gave up on the search, Ken spotted something near the edge of the glow of a streetlight.

A pair of sneakers were visible at the bottom of a niche.

Everything else was a mere silhouette. Ken couldn't discern much about the person lingering across the street.

Probably just a homeless guy trying to stay warm, Ken thought.

As he continued along the sidewalk, an unsettled feeling raised the hairs on the back of his neck. He hoped it was the freezing weather. But the creepy feeling persisted.

Ken headed down the steps to the subway line and the temperature grew warmer.

An image of the sneakers came to mind. It gave him the jitters.

He could picture them. White with a black stripe.

Nike did not make the sneakers.

Ken realized they were Pumas.

Then he tried to place when he had seen Pumas, trying to understand the trepidation he felt merely by the sight of someone getting shelter from the weather.

Belliveau had worn Pumas the first day he'd met him.

It couldn't have been him, Ken decided. *That would be totally crazy.*

Yet, the unsettled feeling didn't escape him. Even as he sat in the subway car as it rattled through tunnels, Ken couldn't shake the uneasy vision from his mind. He felt the crowded subway car closing in on him. It became difficult to breath.

He gasped for air and felt totally ensnared by his new client. Belliveau was turning into a boogeyman.

TWENTY

AFTER a shower and a clean shave, Ken got dressed in pants and a dress shirt. Then he threw on a peacoat and hoofed it over to the restaurant.

Entering the establishment, Ken scanned the place but didn't see Alyson.

She's probably caught up in traffic, he thought.

The restaurant had small tables and plush chairs for intimate dining. Several people were seated at the tables. A large bar ran along the back wall, and it was lined with higher-end stools that matched the dining chairs. Much of the bar was unoccupied. It was still early in the week.

A hostess stood behind a stand, reached into it, and pulled out a few menus.

She watched him curiously, then she asked, "Do you need a table?"

"Can I just grab a seat at the bar?" Ken said, anxiously.

The hostess slid the menus away and forced a smile. "Sure."

"I'm waiting on someone," Ken said, apologetically. "Not certain how long she'll take."

"You can seat yourself," the hostess replied, motioning towards the bar.

"Thanks," Ken said, glancing towards the bar.

As he stepped around the hostess, she smiled flirtatiously, and said, "Come find me if you need a table."

"Sure. Will do."

Ken found a spot at the corner of the bar away from the other patrons. He wanted to put some distance between them, so he and Alyson wouldn't get overheard. He hoped things stayed this way.

There was a small flatscreen television hanging on the wall behind the bar.

While taking in the Celtics game, he waited a few minutes before the bartender ambled over. The place was dead, but the guy didn't seem to be in a rush. He was older, with a stout build and thinning gray hair.

"What can I do for you," the bartender said, without making an introduction.

"I'll go with a gin and tonic," Ken said. "Tanqueray."

The bartender smirked, like he was expecting as much. "Coming up," he said, then he trundled off to the other side of the bar.

Ken pulled out his phone and checked for messages.

There weren't any voicemails or texts. He thought about the next generation phones like Belliveau had purchased and wondered what it would be like in a few years. Everyone would be using text messages, sending and receiving emails on their phones, and the social media craze that was kicking off could become widespread.

He frowned at the thought of all the potential interruptions. Times where a guy could sit at a bar and nurse a drink while taking in the game were coming to an end. All the reports suggested constant interruptions with expectations of regular communications. No break.

The bartender returned and set the drink down on a napkin. "Will you be dining with us tonight?" he asked.

"I'm not sure," Ken said, reaching for the cocktail. "We might grab a table."

The bartender looked at him, confused. His countenance reflected dismay at someone who couldn't make up their mind. Annoyance. A short temper.

"I'm waiting on someone," Ken explained.

"Got it," the bartender said, tossing a towel over his shoulder.

The bartender walked away, and Ken reached for the drink.

He took a sip and set the glass down. Everything from the night before came rushing back at him.

He felt like crap.

Ken figured that he probably still looked horrible.

And thinking about taking another sip from his drink made him feel queasy.

He picked up the glass, lifted it to his mouth, then he set it down without doing anything more than wetting his lips. Ken sat there for a moment, watching the lime as it bobbed between chucks of ice. He wondered if this dinner was a mistake.

He needed to sleep off the effects from the previous night.

Ken had never played around with drugs, and he'd mostly kept his alcohol intake to a minimum. This wasn't something that he could bounce back from with a short passage of time. He needed a long night's rest.

Effervescent bubbles danced upward in the glass, which had become coated in a layer of moisture. He wondered if he should order an appetizer.

The bartender wandered back over. "Anything wrong with your drink?"

"No. It's perfectly fine," Ken said.

"Well, you haven't really touched it."

"Just nursing it until my companion arrives."

"That it?" the bartender questioned.

Ken figured the man had seen people under the weather before. A night out on the town and getting a few sheets to the wind can catch up on a person. He didn't want to indulge the man's suspicions.

Many people were carefree in divulging their problems to a bartender. Ken didn't care to reveal his secrets.

"Yup. That's pretty much it."

"Okay, then."

The bartender turned away, as if dissatisfied that he hadn't heard more.

A few minutes later, Ken heard heels clacking on the floor behind him. He turned and spotted Alyson approaching.

Alyson walked catlike towards him with a devilish look in her eyes. She appeared to have spent time getting herself together before heading out of the office. Her hair was full of body and jounced as she walked, and she wore black lipstick.

"Hey, there," she said, giving him a kiss on the cheek.

"You look great," Ken said.

"Thanks."

Her eyes were slightly glassy, and her words came out mildly slurred. Alyson had apparently imbibed somewhere on her way over.

"Are we getting a table, or slumming it at the bar?" she said.

"Let's get a table," Ken said. "The bartender is a drag."

She looked the bartender over and shrugged. "Okay."

"Do you want to pick a table while I settle up?"

"Sure."

As Alyson headed over to the hostess, Ken settled up the tab with the bartender. The stout man had a big smirk on his face. The guy had watched her walk across the room. Ken figured the bartender was impressed with Alyson. Everyone was taken by her, and Ken figured he was lucky to land a girl like her. Yet, there were many times when he didn't feel so lucky.

She had picked a table by a window and Ken was glad about her choice.

He walked over with his drink in hand and sat down at the table. "This is a good spot," he said.

"You like it?" Alyson said with a flirtatious tone.

"I don't like to get overheard."

"Are you afraid I'll start talking dirty?"

Ken was surprised by her comment. She clearly had stopped for a few cocktails before coming over to the restaurant. Alyson tended to speak indirectly. This was unusual.

"I figured you had something important to say about the office," he said.

"I do. But you go first."

"Afraid I don't have any exciting news. In fact, it might just be the opposite."

A server came over carrying a pitcher of water. She turned their glasses upright and filled them. "My name is Jessica," she said, looking them both over.

"Good evening," Alyson said, kindly.

Jessica looked at Ken's drink on the table. She turned to Alyson, and said, "Would you care for a cocktail?"

Alyson seemed to mull it over. "I'll just go with a house Merlot."

Jessica smiled at the selection. "I'll be right back."

After she stepped away, Ken reached for Alyson's hand. "What's going on with you?"

She caressed his hand for a moment, then she retracted her hand altogether.

"I meant... with your news."

Alyson took a long sip of water. Then she set the glass down and looked him steadily in the eyes. Any sign of inebriation was suddenly gone. "I've been given sort of a promotion."

"A promotion?" Ken repeated, flashing a wide smile.

"Yes."

"Well, that's great."

"I'll be overseeing major crimes."

Ken wasn't sure that he heard her correctly. "Did you say... major crimes?"

Alyson nodded. "Yes."

"My old job?"

"Yes."

"But I thought that Dan was giving that position to—"

"Todd Walton?"

"Yeah."

"He's going into private practice. A firm over in the Seaport District that handles professional liability matters for architects and engineers."

Ken nodded understanding. He took a long swig from his drink.

"You don't sound happy for me," she said.

He looked up. "No. No. It's nothing like that."

"What, then?"

"I'm just surprised. That's all."

"So, you are... *happy* for me?" she asked.

"Yes. Of course I'm happy." He cracked a sly grin.

Ken wanted to reach for her hand and assure her. But the hand he'd held was now under the table and the other glued to the stem of her water glass.

"That's good then," Alyson said.

Jessica returned and placed a glass of wine on the table. She took their orders. Alyson had requested shrimp fra diavolo, and Ken ordered chicken parmesan. When the server walked away, there was a lull in their discussion.

Ken and Alyson fidgeted with their drinks, as if not knowing what to say next.

"So, what's new with you Kenny?" Alyson asked after a moment.

Ken had wanted to tell her everything about the issues with Belliveau. He distrusted the client and suspected something awful had gone down last night. Now, he realized that Alyson potentially had oversight over Belliveau's case. He couldn't confide in her, even if he wanted to tell her everything.

"Nothing much," he finally said.

"You sure?"

"I couldn't tell you anyway."

Anger flittered in her eyes. "Is that how it's going to be?"

"No," Ken said. "Well, actually... to some extent, yes. It is. This does change things."

"How so?"

"It limits what I can say to you."

"Do you really think that I would reveal your private discussions with me to people in the office?"

"No. But you're essentially the third highest person in that office."

"That's not entirely correct."

"You know what I'm saying. There are only a couple people more important than you."

Alyson sat back and considered the comment. "I hadn't thought about it that way."

"You potentially have oversight over my cases. People will come to you seeking advice and direction. It would compromise my client's interests."

"I suppose you're right. It's better not to talk about it at all."

"Agreed."

"*No shop talk,*" she said, chuckling.

Alyson had repeated an adage that Ken used quite often. He laughed and took a sip of his drink. "Things will get interesting," he said.

A server eventually walked over carrying a tray loaded with their orders.

Once the server unloaded their entrees and departed, they tasted the food and were both pleased with the result. This was turning into a decent night. Ken was glad that he hadn't just gone home to bed.

TWENTY-ONE

LATER, as they were working through their meals, Alyson glanced out the window and looked surprised.

Ken peeked out and watched two people ambling down the sidewalk. "Was that..."

Alyson nodded. "Yes. Judge Wexler."

"Who was she with?"

"I'm pretty sure it's Thomas Birnbaum."

"Who's he?"

"A partner at Finley Hoage."

"What's she doing with him?" Ken muttered.

Before Alyson could answer, the judge and lawyer stepped into the restaurant.

"They're coming in here," Ken said.

The lawyer headed for the bar. Ken figured the judge was going to hang up her coat and meet him over there.

"Do you think it's odd that she's with him?" Ken asked.

"My guess is—"

"She's coming over here," Ken said.

TWENTY-TWO

KEN waited to see if the judge was really heading towards their table. She walked rather quickly, but she had a look of anguish on her face. He wondered if she'd suffered a back injury or some other ailment.

Maybe she's been in a car accident, Ken wondered.

Judge Wexler was in her late fifties. She was short and portly. A tweed bucket hat was perched back on the top of her head. Her dark hair was cut at shoulder length and puffed out from beneath the hat. The closer she got to their table, the more the dim light revealed the gray strands in her hair. Wrinkles on her face gave her an aged look beyond her years.

She wore a wool overcoat, and there was a mink fur wrapped around her neck. It wasn't imitation, either. The judge was old-school from a local Irish family and had married a Jewish lawyer, who had done well and was now also a judge.

"She's really headed over here," Ken whispered.

"Kenny..." Alyson began.

The judge sidled up to their table. She huffed to catch her breath and looked at Ken.

Ken stood up. "Judge Wexler, nice to see you."

"Wish I could say the same," she replied.

He was thrown off by the comment. Ken stood there, wondering whether to speak. Judge Wexler remained standing. She appeared to be contemplating what to say next. All the potential conflicts of interest ran through Ken's head, and he feared she'd disclose something about one of his cases.

Judge Wexler turned to Alyson. "Where are my manners?"

the judge said. "Alyson, it's nice to see you. Congratulations on your recent position."

Ken couldn't believe that Alyson's new role had gotten around that fast. The judge had heard about it before him.

"Nice to see you, Judge," Alyson said, but her tone sounded guarded.

"May I have a moment to speak with Kenny?" Judge Wexler asked Alyson.

"Sure."

Alyson looked at Ken. "I'll just get a dessert menu and look it over while the two of you chat."

There was a hint of caution in Alyson's eyes. Ken suspected that she wanted to warn him about something. He felt he was missing something. News traveled fast around town in certain circles. Leaving the D.A.'s Office had left him out of the loop.

"Where do you want to talk," Ken said, motioning to the bar.

"Let's just borrow a table," Judge Wexler said.

She trundled over to an empty table, away from the other diners, without asking permission from the hostess. Judge Wexler sat down, but she didn't remove her coat.

Ken took a seat across from her. "How are you doing?" he said.

"Wish I was better."

Now, he really wondered what was going on.

She cracked a smile. "The confusion on your face tells me you haven't heard the news yet."

"What news?"

"Kenny, I got picked up." Her tone sounded motherly.

"*Picked up?*" he repeated, confused.

"It was a DUI charge."

Ken sat back astounded. "I don't know what to say."

"Say that you'll represent me," she said, placidly. It was a reassuring tone, like doing so was perfectly kosher.

He considered the request. "I'm not sure that I can."

Judge Wexler canted her head and smiled condescendingly. "You're worried about the potential conflicts?"

Ken nodded. "Yes."

"That won't be a problem."

"Well, I've never encountered a situation like this," Ken said. "I'd have to research it before we can talk any further. You handled post-trial motions in a big case that is now up on appeal."

Judge Wexler nodded, understandingly. "That case is what this is all about."

"What are you saying?"

"I'm saying that I was set up by the police. They're mad about those decisions."

"Judge, if that case is what this is all about…"

She held up a hand to silence him.

"We're not in court right now," he protested.

"Relax. I am going on administrative leave until this is all worked out." Judge Wexler motioned to the fancy lawyer at the bar. "I've retained competent civil counsel, as you can see. We have already discussed who to handle the criminal aspect. It's merely fortuitous that we ran into each other here."

Ken couldn't believe he'd been the subject of such a high-level discussion.

"Surprised your ears weren't burning," Judge Wexler said.

"Judge don't the rules include even the impression of impropriety?"

"That's really more about potential issues when a judge is presiding over a case. I've already been told that this wouldn't be an issue."

"But—"

"I'm entitled to a defense," she snapped.

Ken was taken aback. He merely shook his head and waited for the moment to pass.

"I'm sorry," she said. "I didn't mean to take it out on you."

"No," Ken said. "No apologies necessary. This must be a difficult situation."

"So, will you take my case?" she asked, hopefully.

"Aside from conflicts, there are other things to consider."

"Like what?" she asked. And her interest genuinely appeared piqued.

"This is a high-profile case. It will get into the press."

"Understood."

"You need the best result. Have you thought about someone with more experience as a criminal defense lawyer? An attorney specializing in DUI?"

Judge Wexler shook her head. "I don't want one of those guys defending *me*."

"I've only been on this side of things for about six months."

She waved her hand, dismissively. "That's exactly why *we* want you."

Ken glanced over at the bar. They had considered all the angles. This wasn't a happenstance discussion from an impromptu meeting. It was a carefully planned strategy.

"Okay," he finally said. "We'll get you an engagement letter in the morning."

"Thank you, Kenny."

He smiled kindly. "You're welcome."

"I'll let you get back to Alyson."

Ken stood and started back for his table.

"Kenny," the judge called after him.

He turned and faced her. "Yes."

"You be careful now. They're bound to come after you next."

TWENTY-THREE

KEN slept late and woke up feeling refreshed. He got dressed and headed into the office for an easy paperwork day. He didn't have any court appearances or depositions, and there weren't any pressing deadlines. It was going to be a nice, stress-free day.

At the office, he settled behind his desk with a cup of coffee. He checked emails, then he started drafting the police misconduct complaint in Belliveau's civil case.

There was a rap on his door, followed by Mickey poking his head in. "Ken Dwyer!" Mickey said. "There's the man of the hour."

Ken sat back in his chair, confused.

Mickey stepped inside, leaving the door wide open.

"What's up?" Ken said.

"You made the headlines," Mickey said.

Mickey tossed the Boston Herald onto Ken's desk.

A large black and white photograph of Judge Wexler was plastered to the front page. The headline read: JUDGE NABBED FOR DRUNK DRIVING.

Ken perused the article. It talked about the arrest and the judge's background on the bench. Then it mentioned that she had handled post-trial motions in a case where the Boston Police had withheld evidence from the prosecutor and the defense. It stated that the criminal case was under appeal and the legal community anticipated the case would be remanded for a new trial.

A small picture of Ken appeared in the lower righthand corner of the page. It stated that the former prosecutor is rumored to be handling the judge's defense. Then the piece went on to talk about bail and the arraignment, which was scheduled for early the next week.

Ken made a note to put the arraignment on his calendar. He also remembered that he needed to get an engagement agreement to the judge.

"Why didn't you tell me about this?" Mickey said.

"This came up kind of fast," Ken said, apologetically.

Mickey stood there, red-faced from booze and chuckled.

"I haven't been formally engaged, either."

"Well, get a nice fat retainer."

"So, you're not mad that I didn't come to you first?"

"Heck, no."

"What's the deal?"

"Just thought you'd be eager to share a juicy tidbit with me. Rather than my learning about it in the morning's paper."

Ken shrugged. "Only talked to her last night."

"Uh-huh."

"The press got a hold of it pretty quick. Wonder how they found out so fast."

"Her team leaked it to them," Mickey said. "She probably has someone lined up to handle a judicial misconduct matter."

Ken was surprised at how fast Mickey had processed the situation.

"You doubt me?" asked Mickey.

"No. I'm shocked at what a quick study you are."

Mickey grinned. "This is going to call for a cold one at lunch. On me."

"You've got it."

As Mickey turned to leave, Ken said, "She hired Finley Hoage."

The old trial lawyer smirked. "Could have figured as much. This will drain their resources fast. We'll be the least important to pay. Better make it a 10K retainer."

"Got it."

Mickey left. Ken stopped what he was doing to get the engagement agreement together. Then he called over to Finley

Hoage and got put through to Tom Birnbaum, who decided that the engagement letter should be sent through his office.

Birnbaum then asked to be included in all discussions and communications with Judge Wexler. They were circling the wagons and Ken already felt that he was on the outside looking in.

TWENTY-FOUR

LATER, the day shifted into afternoon and Ken had completed the factual background section on the new lawsuit.

With cases like this, providing detailed facts were crucial to surviving dispositive motions. The claims themselves were pattern and formulaic, but drafting the facts takes time. He planned to finish up the pleading and set it aside overnight. Then he'd give it another review before sending it to the client.

Ken had decided to file the lawsuit in Suffolk Superior Court because the two key defendants who had spearheaded the search were with the Boston police.

He decided to take a quick break and got up to fetch a cup of water.

Returning to his office, Ken stretched out his back and sat down. He checked his email and noticed one from Belliveau.

The subject line read: *Lawsuit?*

Ken opened the email and there wasn't a message.

He wondered if Belliveau had hit send by mistake before completing a full email. After waiting a few minutes, Ken realized the email he received was what Belliveau had intended to send to him. It was impersonal and unprofessional.

The tactic stirred anger. Ken's heart raced and his veins pulsated.

What's this guy's problem? Ken thought.

He'd just told Belliveau the day before not to expect to see the lawsuit right away. This guy was going to hound him every minute, monopolize his time, and act like Ken didn't have any other cases. He thought about cutting Belliveau loose, but he didn't want to stir things up with Mickey.

The email was distracting, and Ken lost the incentive to continue working on the complaint.

Ken went through other emails, responding to clients who treated him respectfully.

Hoping to take his mind off the frustration with Belliveau, he headed into the hallway and made his way to the back of the suite. There were workstations in an area with windows overlooking the back parking lot.

Ken walked over to a copy and mailing station and checked his slot for incoming mail. There were a few notices from courts, and he planned to read through everything when he got back to his desk.

Turning to leave, Ken ran into Mickey who had ambled into the back room. "Hey, boss," Ken said.

Mickey nodded. Then he walked over to the mail station.

As Ken walked off, Mickey called out. "Please move your car out of the back lot tonight."

"Sure thing."

"It's been back there too long. The landlord busted my chops about it."

"Consider it done."

Ken headed towards his office and found Pat sitting at her desk with the phone cradled in one ear. She looked annoyed and waved for him to step over to her desk. She was listening to someone rattle on the other end of the line.

As Ken approached, she told the caller, "Hold on."

Then she hit the mute button and looked up at him, pleadingly.

"What's going on?" Ken said.

"It's *him*," she said, exasperated.

"*Him?*" But even as Ken mouthed the words, he knew who she meant.

"Belliveau," Pat said. "He's called three times today. You told me not to disturb you, but he just keeps calling. And he doesn't take no for an answer. Keeps asking what you're doing."

"Okay, you can put him through."

Ken walked into this office and felt his anger rising.

He reached for the phone and answered professionally. "This is Ken Dwyer."

"Did you get my email?" Belliveau said.

"Your email?"

"The one looking for an update about the lawsuit."

"Look, I didn't get a request for an update," Ken snapped. "I got a rather unprofessional email with one word written in the subject line and a question mark. That isn't a request for an update. In fact, I don't know what that is."

"Sorry," Belliveau said. And he sounded apologetic.

Ken didn't offer an olive branch.

"I didn't want to bother you," Belliveau said after a moment.

Ken thought the comment was ludicrous. That's all the guy did was pester him and his staff. Something about this guy made Ken's blood boil. An arrogance mixed with entitlement. However, he kept his cool. "That's fine," Ken said.

"I've tried to call," Belliveau said. "Seems like you're avoiding me."

"I've been working on *your* case," Ken carped.

"Oh, I didn't know."

"Drafting something like that takes time and concentration. I don't like to be distracted unless it's an emergency."

"Understood. Sorry to bother you."

"Okay, then."

"When do you think I can take a look at it?"

"Tomorrow."

Ken couldn't believe the guy. Most clients just wait until the lawyer sends over the draft complaint, and then they just quickly peruse it to confirm the factual assertions.

"Sounds good."

"I'll send it over tomorrow. Talk to you later."

"Sure."

Ken went to hang up the phone and the guy kept talking.

"Just want you to know that I appreciate everything,"

Belliveau said. "I just wanted to make sure that we're still on track. I know that you're a busy guy. You've got bigger fish to fry. That's all."

He's talking about the Wexler case, Ken realized.

Belliveau had seen the news and wondered if his case was getting neglected. It hadn't.

"Take care," Ken said, then he quickly hung up the phone before Belliveau could say another word.

Ken felt a wave of anger consume him. Then, he punched a hole in the wall.

TWENTY-FIVE

THE DAY transitioned into evening and Ken hadn't heard from Alyson about plans for the evening. He was about to call her when a crash echoed from out back.

The sound resembled the noise typically heard from the dumpster lids slamming closed during trash removal. It was too late in the day for a trash truck to be making the rounds.

Ken shut down the office, then he left for the day.

Stepping into the cold, he hoofed it along the sidewalk and down the alley leading behind the building. The darkness left him with an eerie feeling as he moved through the shadows. Much of the alleyway was so dark, he couldn't make out what was in front of him.

Finally, he reached the other side and stepped into the parking area. A light post illuminated the area.

All the cars had cleared out, except for his Volkswagen.

Ken walked over and his stomach dropped. The entire front end of his car was completely caved in. Damage extended into the engine compartment.

Fluids leaked from the undercarriage and ran over the macadam.

"What a mess," he muttered.

He called the police and reported a hit-and-run accident.

About fifteen minutes later a patrol car arrived. Two officers climbed out of the car and Ken was glad that he didn't recognize either one. It was probably better to deal with people who didn't know him.

An older officer asked him what happened, and Ken

explained. The cop had a gruff demeanor, but he appeared to be taking this by the numbers. They went through the standard routine, then the younger police officer climbed into the squad car and slid behind the wheel.

"You should report this to your insurance carrier," the older cop said.

"I'll plan to."

"Can you come by the precinct in the next couple of days and fill out a police report?" the cop said.

"Sure." Ken followed the officer back to the police car.

"That would be appreciated," the cop said, climbing into the cruiser.

Ken stood beside the passenger door, wondering if anything would ever come of this.

The old cop lowered his window. "We'll check to see when the last time the dumpster was emptied."

"Thanks."

"Something tells me it wasn't the trash truck. Those guys have plenty of insurance and typically report stuff like this."

"Do you think you'll ever find who's responsible?" Ken asked.

"You tell me, counselor."

Ken was amazed the cop knew he was a lawyer.

"Don't look surprised," the cop said. "People are bound to recognize you when your face is plastered all over the morning's paper."

His comment made sense.

"You'll look into this, though?" Ken asked, sheepishly.

"Sure," the cop said. "Sure, we'll get right on this. We love to help those who sue the police and get bad guys out of trouble. Sure we'll look right into this."

Then, he raised the window and flashed a sardonic grin, as the cruiser meandered out of the parking lot onto the roadway.

Ken stood by and aimlessly waited for a tow truck. He was starting to feel like public enemy number one of the Boston police.

TWENTY-SIX

THE FOLLOWING week Ken found himself seated in the conference room across from Belliveau. He had sent the draft complaint to the kid. Ordinarily, a client just looked it over and pointed out a few factual corrections and the lawsuit got filed.

Belliveau had wanted to meet in person, and they ended up discussing the entire pleading.

"This looks good," Belliveau said after perusing the document.

"Okay," Ken said. "We'll get it filed."

Ken stood up, signaling that the meeting had ended.

"Hold on," Belliveau barked.

What is it now? Ken thought.

He sat back down and looked at Belliveau.

"I've got a thought on this," Belliveau said, pointing at the complaint.

"What?" Ken wasn't in the mood for a client playing the role of a jailhouse lawyer.

"This needs a claim for civil conspiracy," Belliveau said. Then, he flashed a wide, cocky smile, like he was the smartest guy in the city, and his lawyer had overlooked an angle.

Ken sat back in his chair and shook his head.

"Why not?" Belliveau said.

"Because you are trying to make this too complicated. It's a basic warrantless search."

"They were conspiring against me," Belliveau complained.

"You need to present facts in support of a claim," Ken said. "We don't have details of what was going on in their minds."

"But—"

"It will get dismissed," Ken said, curtly.

"Really?"

"Yes. And fighting that will tie up the entire case."

"But can't you allege facts based upon information and belief?"

The kid had done some research, probably had seen a few lawsuits online. Ken didn't feel like explaining basic legal procedure. The meeting had already taken too long.

"You need a basis for even making an allegation based upon information and belief…"

"They were out to get me!" Belliveau complained.

Ken shook his head. "That won't fly."

Belliveau's face turned red with anger. He clenched his teeth.

"Listen, we file the lawsuit as we have it," Ken said. "If there is any discovery to support another claim, then we'll discuss it. You don't want to get a claim dismissed early on. The better practice is to obtain discovery and file a motion to amend the complaint."

"Okay," Belliveau said. "As long as you'll consider it."

"Are we done here?" asked Ken.

"Well, I wanted to talk to you about the other matter."

"Other matter?" Ken said.

"Yeah. The firearms case that we discussed."

Ken listened while Belliveau told him about his divorce matter. The divorce court judge had issued a restraining order for a year. It had been lifted, but there was an order in place to sell a collection of firearms.

"They are all legit," Belliveau said. "I have a Firearm Identification Card."

"So, what's the deal?" Ken considered him. "You want them back?"

"Heck no," Belliveau said.

"Then what?"

"We are supposed to split the money from the sale of the firearms. They've all been turned over to a dealer in Revere."

"I'm not following."

"The dealer is selling them way below market value."

"What's in it for him?" Ken asked.

"He's supposed to get a commission. But I think he's reporting them being sold lower than the actual sale to make a bigger profit."

Ken pondered the comment. "It would be a dangerous game. They have to keep records on every sale. All you'd have to do is find the buyers from federal forms and contact them to see how much they paid for the guns. The sales prices will either match up or they won't."

"Another possibility is that he sold them to friends cheap. The friends turned around and sold them."

"You could figure that out with a few quick depositions. Still a lot of risk."

"Well, I'm willing to take it."

"It's not your license on the line," Ken said, sternly.

Belliveau's expression froze, as he registered the severity of a lawyer's ethical obligations. Ken wouldn't just file a lawsuit willy-nilly. It was good for the young man to grasp this.

"What do you need?" Belliveau said.

"Documentation on the purchases of all the firearms," Ken said. "Receipts for the ones sold to date by the dealer. And research on what those guns should have sold for."

"I can probably get all of that."

"We also need photographs and an affidavit from you on the condition of…"

"That part's easy. I bought them all brand new."

"Then the market value will be easier to establish."

Belliveau stood up. He was grinning happily, almost too happily.

Ken rose from his chair and reached for the complaint.

"Can I hold on to this?" Belliveau said.

"Sure." But Ken didn't understand why the kid needed it, or why a client would want a draft copy of a pleading. "I'll walk you out."

Ken led Belliveau to the elevator bank. "Mickey will want a retainer for the new matter."

Belliveau looked at him askance. "But you have a retainer."

"We took a retainer for the criminal matter and burned through it."

"You have one for the civil case," Belliveau said.

"That's for expenses," Ken said. "We won't touch that, except to pay for out-of-pocket expenses, like the filing fee, deposition transcripts, and experts."

"Understood," Belliveau said. "Send over the agreement and I'll get you a retainer."

Ken shook Belliveau's hand. Then the kid got into the elevator with a spring in his step.

He's a little too chipper for my comfort, Ken thought.

There was something more to this second case than the client had disclosed. Probably the same with the police misconduct case, and he was about to file the complaint.

TWENTY-SEVEN

THE NEXT morning, Ken found himself standing before a judge, and next to a judge, in the Boston Municipal Court. It was a newer courthouse with veneer tables, bench, and witness box. The courtroom was packed with spectators and the press.

Judge Wexler was fidgety and nervous.

Ken had anticipated she might be an overbearing client, but it was the exact opposite. She was submissive and contrite, almost to the point of appearing apologetic. He'd also expected Thomas Birnbaum to try and direct the criminal matter. But that wasn't the case, either.

Tom sat quietly in the pews and hadn't offered any pointers.

Alyson and a young prosecutor stood at the prosecution table. She was letting him take the lead, but she clearly was in attendance to show support from the higher-ups in the D.A.'s Office.

Maureen Honeycutt sat behind the polished bench reviewing the court file. She was a Black judge who had gone to Harvard for undergraduate school and Yale for law school.

Judge Honeycutt looked up and considered the lawyers and the defendant. She didn't appear pleased with the situation. No judge wants to preside over a politically charged matter. But Ken got the feeling that her consternation went deeper. She was displeased with something in the file. Honeycutt had worked hard to get to her station in life, and she clearly frowned upon public officials getting themselves into hot water.

"How does the defendant plead?" Judge Honeycutt finally said.

"Not guilty, Your Honor," Ken replied.

"Mr. Dwyer, I'd like to hear directly from the defendant."

Ken leaned over to Judge Wexler. "Go ahead."

"Not… guilty," she muttered. "Your Honor."

Judge Honeycutt nodded. Then, she looked at the prosecutor, and said, "The plea has been entered. Do you have anything else for us today?"

"We have Your Honor."

"What is it?"

"The Commonwealth would like to address bail."

"Bail?" Ken blurted.

"Mr. Dwyer, please let him finish," Judge Honeycutt said. "Continue."

"It has come to our attention that the defendant has a prior offense," the prosecutor said, sounding snarky. "The Commonwealth seeks to revoke bail."

People in the gallery gasped in unison.

"Revoke bail?" Ken barked.

Judge Honeycutt glanced at him. "Let's settle down, counselor."

"What's this all about?" Ken whispered to his client.

Wexler looked dumbfounded.

"What are the circumstances?" Judge Honeycutt asked the prosecutor.

"Apparently, the defendant had a DUI out of state when she was in college. The conviction was expunged, so we didn't catch it when she posted bail."

"This shouldn't count," Judge Wexler said to Ken.

Ken couldn't believe what he was hearing from a client who was a sitting judge. Massachusetts had a lifetime look back for DUI charges, and the state considered any conviction in factoring a prior offense. A second offense included a mandatory jail sentence, unless an inpatient alcohol treatment was ordered during sentencing.

"Counselor?" Judge Honeycutt asked Ken.

"Your Honor," Ken replied. "The maximum sentence for a

second offense is sixty days. This court can't possibly hold my client in jail while she awaits a trial. This is nothing more than a political stunt. I'd like to know the last five times they asked for no bail when the first offense was over twenty years ago."

Judge Honeycutt nodded, as if she agreed with the defense.

The judge straightened up. Then, she looked sternly at the prosecutor. "My review of the file reflects that the defendant refused a breathalyzer. This means she is subject to an automatic suspension of her driving privileges. She, therefore, does not present a danger to the public. *If* you get a conviction, we will address jail time during sentencing."

"But, Your Honor..." the prosecutor pled.

Judge Honeycutt eyeballed him harshly.

Alyson grabbed his arm, indicating that he should be quiet.

The young lawyer didn't know when to stop. "Your Honor, we—"

"Enough!" Judge Honeycutt bellowed.

The prosecutor lowered his head, embarrassed by the chastisement.

"The defendant shall remain on personal recognizance bail," Judge Honeycutt said. "She is prohibited from driving, unless further ordered by this court. Anything else?"

"Your Honor," the prosecutor said.

"I've made my ruling."

"Well, I was hoping to schedule the next event."

"You'll get sent a notice like everybody else." Honeycutt moved the file aside and grabbed another one.

Ken shoved his notepad and a manilla folder into his briefcase.

Judge Wexler stood beside him, waiting for instruction.

The young prosecutor stood there, like he had something else to say, while Alyson stepped around him and moved towards the gate.

A massive group of people cleared out of the gallery. Most of them were there to watch this hearing and only a few stragglers were left to be heard in their own cases.

Judge Honeycutt caught the prosecutor out of the corner of her eye. "That will be all."

He looked chagrinned. Then, he sheepishly packed up his bag.

Ken gently touched his client on the arm. "Come on," he said. "Let's get through the crowd and find a meeting room. We can talk about next steps and wait out the press."

She nodded and followed him to the gate.

Running into Alyson, Ken smiled and tried not to make a scene. He wanted to gripe about her not giving him warning about appearing at the hearing. She wore her best suit, a black Anne Taylor jacket and skirt with a cream blouse. She carried a tan, wool coat, and her hair looked like she had just stepped out of a salon.

She's here for the press coverage, Ken concluded.

TWENTY-EIGHT

KEN followed a throng of gadflies through a set of double doors and found an empty meeting room outside the courtroom.

He ushered his client inside the room and closed the door. Then he set his briefcase on the table.

Judge Wexler took a seat, while Ken paced the small room waiting for Birnbaum. The high-priced civil lawyer had apparently gotten lost in the crowd. Ken wondered how long it would take the attorney to find them.

"Maybe you should call him," Ken offered.

Judge Wexler nodded, and the flesh on her neck jiggled. She pulled her cellphone out of a coat pocket and flipped it open. Then she searched for Birnbaum in her contacts. The lawyer was clearly a high priority in her life right now. She hit a button.

"Tom?" she said a moment later.

"Where are you guys?" Ken faintly heard Birnbaum reply.

"There's a meeting room just outside the courtroom," she said. "We're inside. Why don't you come join us?"

She ended the call and the two of them waited for Birnbaum to arrive.

Ken couldn't think of anything to say that would help ease his client's burden. The room was small, and the corners of the veneer table were peeled back and worn. There wasn't a sadder place for a superior court judge to wind up, other than a holding cell downtown.

A few minutes later, Birnbaum entered the room looking flabbergasted.

He took a seat and slumped in his chair. "There's a mob

out there," Birnbaum said, exasperated. "And your girlfriend is yacking it up with the press."

Judge Wexler stared at Ken, looking disappointed in him.

Ken waited for the moment to pass. "Sorry about that."

"It's not your fault Ken," the judge said. "But I really wish you'd given us notice that she'd be in attendance."

"She didn't give *me* any notice," Ken griped.

Birnbaum waved a hand dismissively. "Wouldn't have changed a thing."

Judge Wexler nodded. "Right. Let's not start fighting amongst ourselves. We should think about next steps."

Ken took a seat at the table. "I like to flesh out potential action items at a time like this. Then we sit on the options and make a final decision later."

Birnbaum and the judge nodded their heads in agreement.

"Tell me about this other arrest," Ken said.

"Well, there's not much to say. I was in college and had gone out with some friends. It really was a long time ago. I'd let it slip my mind."

"It makes the situation a little more severe," Ken said. "Typically, a lawyer gets popped for a DUI and it's a driver's license suspension and a slap on the wrist. A conviction for a second offense would come with an inpatient treatment at a minimum." He looked at Birnbaum. "How would that impact her position?"

A dire look crossed Birnbaum's face. He locked glances with the judge and her countenance reflected anguish over the thought of stepping down from the bench in disgrace.

Judge Wexler bent over and shook her head in sorrow.

Ken placed a hand on her shoulder, but he didn't say anything. Hollow words couldn't assuage her displeasure.

She looked up at him. "We have to beat this, Kenny."

"I know. But cases like this usually start out with the prosecution gung-ho for a conviction. The longer the case sits in the system, the more they become open to a reasonable disposition. If you try to strike too fast, you don't get anywhere."

"I think what she's trying to say," Birnbaum cut in. "We need an immediate trial date."

"You'll lose the option for a disposition without a finding," Ken cautioned. "Cases like this aren't a slam dunk."

"My life will be over if this goes on too long."

"It will be disrupted," Ken said. "If you lose, it will be over."

Birnbaum stood up. "I'm afraid she's right."

Judge Wexler stood up. "Get us the soonest trial date. Then prepare like hell."

She turned away. Birnbaum held the door, then the two of them stepped into bedlam without Ken. They were putting her entire career in his hands.

***

AFTER the door closed and shut out the cacophony from the hallway, Ken sat in the small room alone and contemplated the latest developments.

A sitting superior court judge's reputation was in his hands.

He preferred to navigate a criminal case through the system. He'd seen how things develop from a prosecutor's standpoint and as a defense attorney. The longer a case sat in the system, the more likely another prosecutor would pick it up and agree to a fair disposition.

Judge Wexler had retained pricey private counsel to strategize every step of the way.

Ken wondered if the lawyer she had chosen was up to the task. Civil lawyers didn't understand the intricacies of criminal practice.

He wanted to call Alyson and unload. Then, he realized that he could never talk to her about this case. A wall ran down the middle of their relationship, cordoning off discussion. He wondered if they could survive her new promotion.

Leaning his head back, he fell into a quasi-state of sleep. It was something he'd learned in the military. You grabbed some shuteye whenever the opportunity presented itself.

Ken felt drained from the stress of the hearing.

He waited and waited, partially asleep.

Eventually, he snapped awake. Ken gathered himself and stepped into an empty hallway. Everyone had cleared out and he'd dodged the media circus. There was a level of solace in walking through the deserted courthouse.

But on some level, it felt like a defeat. A misstep from the client's past made the stakes higher. Now, he had to pull a rabbit out of his hat.

TWENTY-NINE

RETURNING to the office, Ken stepped out of the elevator and was met by Pat staring at him. She looked concerned.

"You need to see this," she said.

He approached her workstation, and she handed him a stack of pleadings.

"These came today," she said.

"Bad?" He reached for the papers.

Pat nodded. "I took a peek."

Ken glanced at the top document. It was a motion to dismiss Belliveau's police misconduct case. He flipped through the documents and stopped. "A short order notice?" he said.

She nodded again. "Yup. The hearing is scheduled for next week."

"The rules give you fourteen days to get an opposition to the other side," Ken complained. "I've got about half that time. I can't believe this was granted."

"There's politics in play," Pat said.

Ken headed to his office and shut the door. He read through the entire stack of documents. The argument seeking dismissal was surprising, and he contemplated whether his client had given him the complete dope. Guys like Belliveau never divulged the full story.

He pulled out his Dictaphone and started preparing the opposition, as streetlights cut on and staff left the office for the day.

THIRTY

THE NEXT week Ken found himself seated at counsel table with Belliveau by his side. They waited for the judge to take the bench. The kid wasn't dressed for court; he wore a gray hoodie and jeans.

The old courtroom was set up with the plaintiff's table in front near the large oak bench, and two defense tables behind it. Robert Boyle sat at the defense table with two associates. He was an aggressive insurance defense lawyer, known for having a sharp tongue.

Boyle's entire approach for this motion was extremely aggressive. Ken got the feeling that he'd taken such an approach to impress the client. The lawyer wasn't known for handling police misconduct cases, so this case was likely a new opportunity. It would get Boyle's undivided attention.

Ken expected that opposing counsel would swamp him with discovery requests if the case survived this motion.

A side door squeaked open, then Judge Heather McIntyre entered the courtroom.

The bailiff called out, "All rise!"

Everyone at the counsel tables stood up.

There were a few lawyers and a client or two seated on the oak pews in the gallery, waiting for their motions to be heard. They scrambled to their feet.

Judge McIntyre was average height with short blonde hair and a rather Nordic appearance, with a small nose and attractive features. Her robe dragged on the floor as she walked towards the bench.

She glanced around the courtroom, then smiled, "You may be seated."

Turning to the sessions clerk, the judge asked what matter was first on the list. He read the case caption for our case aloud. Then the judge reached for a file from the stack of matters on her desk. After a quick review of the pleadings, she nodded then looked up.

"Can I have the parties introduce themselves, starting with counsel for the plaintiff?"

Ken stood up. "Kenneth Dwyer for the plaintiff."

"Good afternoon, Mr. Dwyer." The judge smiled kindly, as if she liked him.

"With me today..." Ken said, motioning. "My client, Trevor Belliveau."

Belliveau stood up and flashed an arrogant grin, as though he figured he could date the judge if they had met under different circumstances. This apparently wasn't lost on her.

"Mr. Belliveau," she said with a nod, and forced a smile.

Judge McIntyre quickly turned her attention to the lawyers at the defense tables.

"Robert Boyle for the defendants," Boyle said, rising from his chair. His voice bellowed with an arrogant tone. "Judge, with me today are *my* two associates... Kristin Ward and Colleen Baxter."

Ward looked like she was from Connecticut and Baxter was a local girl who had grown up in Dorchester and played basketball at Boston College. Everybody around town knew her and liked her. Ken was surprised she had chosen to work at Boyle's firm.

He was known as a dean of the insurance defense community, but he had a reputation of being difficult to work under.

"Also," Boyle added. "Lieutenant O'Malley is here from the Boston Police Department."

Boyle spoke with a thick Boston accent, and he motioned towards the gallery. A tall man in a gray trench coat stood up and nodded at the judge. He had thick gray hair and resembled a Boston politician.

"Well then," the judge said. "You may all be seated."

Everyone sat down in unison.

"We're here for the defendants' motion to dismiss," the judge said. "Let's hear from counsel for the defense."

Boyle stood up and walked towards a podium, positioned between the two defense tables. He carried a notepad and a stack of pleadings.

He set his materials down, then he cleared his throat. "Judge, it might help if I provide you with some of the factual background."

Judge McIntyre nodded.

"The central issue is that the plaintiff didn't live at the dwelling where the search took place," Boyle said. "He lived with his girlfriend in Revere."

"I see you included quite a bit of material with your motion."

"Correct," Boyle said. "The plaintiff has overnight parking tickets in Revere. Officers investigating a string of pharmacy burglaries have submitted affidavits, stating the plaintiff lives in Revere."

"What about the tools seized at the aunt's house?" asked Judge McIntyre.

"No expectation of privacy," Boyle said matter-of-factly.

The judge sat back in her chair and frowned at him.

Ken worried the hearing wouldn't go well for the plaintiff. His concerns related to a judge allowing the motion for a short order hearing when there really wasn't a good basis for the request. It had the air of favoritism. Now, he was beginning to wonder.

"How so?" the judge said after a moment.

"The aunt owns the dwelling, the plaintiff does not live there, and..."

"Mr. Boyle, are you telling me that if the plaintiff stored his tools in an isolated location in the house—"

"That's disputed," Boyle cut in. "The officers found the possessions commingled."

"Disputed?" The judge looked at Boyle askance.

He paused, realizing his faux paus.

"I'd like to hear from the plaintiff on this," she said.

Ken stood up and presented from his table. "Your Honor, the address issue is merely a ruse. The plaintiff has his car registered at the house where the search took place, he has a lease, we have an affidavit from the aunt saying that he lives there."

The judge nodded and smiled as if amused.

"He visits the girlfriend on occasion," Ken continued. "They aren't even in an exclusive relationship."

"What about the storage of items in the basement."

"Their position relates to boxes in the general basement area. We take the position that the plaintiff had his own dedicated space where he kept business records, athletic equipment, etc. However, this court need not get into a dispute about that space."

The judge grinned. "Tell us why."

"Because the items seized all came from a storage locker that the plaintiff had brought to the property and used exclusively for his tools. It's all in the affidavits from the plaintiff and the aunt."

"Very well," Judge McIntyre said. "Anything else."

"Just that the case law doesn't even support the defendants' theory. A person doesn't have to have items seized from a primary residence in order to have an expectation of privacy. There is case law about hotel rooms, college apartments, crash pads, etc."

The judge turned her attention to defense counsel. "Mr. Boyle?"

He looked angry and just shook his head in defeat.

Ken wondered if an associate or a backroom lawyer had come up with the theories. Perhaps Boyle had run with them not knowing the vulnerability of them because he didn't practice criminal defense, and he probably hadn't much experience in police misconduct matters.

An associate stood up and leaned over, whispering something to Boyle.

"We have a few other arguments," Boyle said.

The judge looked at Ken. "Counselor?"

"There has been a proliferation of motions to dismiss in recent years," Ken said. "A motion to dismiss is typically directed at the four corners of the complaint. It rarely relies upon attached documents and information outside of the complaint. Defense lawyers have started using early motions for summary judgment and disguising them as motions to dismiss. We have a stack of pleadings here with numerous affidavits, parking tickets, and all sorts of documents that speak beyond the four corners of the complaint."

Judge McIntyre nodded, following along.

"The rules of civil procedure allow the court to consider a motion to dismiss with attachments and handle it as a motion for summary judgment. Aside from the search and seizure arguments that we discussed, the motion deals with disputed facts, which have been presented through counter affidavits."

"And?" the judge asked.

"We feel that you should deny the motion in its entirety and with prejudice. And you should handle it as a motion for summary judgment, precluding them from rearguing the same points later."

The judge looked at Boyle. "Response?"

"Judge, this should be handled as a motion to dismiss as filed..."

"Mr. Boyle, you filed this for a short order hearing. And you submitted copious documents and affidavits speaking to issues far outside the facts plead in the complaint. You didn't allow the plaintiff any discovery. You didn't allow the plaintiff much time to respond. Somehow, the plaintiff did respond in full. You've had your opportunity."

"But Judge..." Now, he was leaning on the podium, almost draped over it in defeat.

"I'm denying your motion in it is entirety with prejudice. And I'm taking it as a motion for summary judgment. You will not reargue these points again. However, you are free to file a motion for summary judgment, after some discovery has taken place, based upon separate issues."

"Judge, I'd really like to…"

"That will be all." Judge McIntyre broke off eye contact and moved the file to the side. Then she reached for another file.

"Let's go," Ken said to Belliveau, shoving his notepad into his briefcase and turning to the door with his overcoat in hand.

Belliveau sat in his seat looking dumbfounded.

"Now," Ken snapped.

Ken broke for the door, while Belliveau slowly heeded his instructions. Defense counsel lingered at their table, as if trying to construct another argument in hope of convincing the judge to revisit her position.

The last thing Ken wanted was to be present when they thought of something more to say. He wanted to be long gone before they could revive their argument.

THIRTY-ONE

KEN waited in the hallway outside the courtroom for Belliveau. The kid didn't come out. The defense lawyers had also stayed behind.

He feared a bailiff would step into the corridor and summon him back into the courtroom.

Walking over to the elevator bank, Ken planned to get out of there before anything drastic could happen. He'd follow up with Belliveau later if the kid didn't get his act together. An elevator dinged and he saw the arrow above the doors light up.

Just as Ken walked over to the lift, his client came lumbering out of the courtroom.

Ken stepped into the elevator and held the door open.

Belliveau scooted inside and looked around at the occupants, who were headed down to the lobby from the upper levels. Most were lawyers. A few looked like *pro se* criminal defendants. There was one guy who was probably a clerk in the courthouse stepping out for a late lunch.

The kid seemed to know that he shouldn't get into a discussion about the case.

"We'll talk outside," Ken said, reenforcing the need for confidentiality.

"Sure." Belliveau shrugged. "We could have grabbed a room."

"Outside," Ken reiterated.

The elevator jockeyed down to the lobby, and everyone unloaded and quickly headed for the exit. Ken stepped to the side of the throng and let them pass. He wriggled into his overcoat.

"I've got to grab my phone from security," Belliveau said.

"Okay, I'll meet you outside."

Ken walked across the lobby, then stepped outside into a frigid afternoon.

He waited on the courthouse steps for Belliveau to catch up. The brick courtyard was covered in a layer of snow.

Ken watched as people came and went. Some looked pleased with the results of their afternoon motion sessions. Others appeared dismayed. A few attorneys walked along with stoic faces, not revealing happiness or displeasure. Those lawyers were mostly from posh law firms, where they got paid exorbitant fees whether they won or lost.

Belliveau eventually ventured outside. He walked up to Ken. "Hey, do you want to grab a coffee and talk about what happened today?"

Ken was reluctant to meet with the guy informally after what he suspected happened the last time they were together. He paused and didn't answer.

"Well?" Belliveau said.

"This will only take a moment," Ken finally replied.

Belliveau shivered. "But it's freezing out here."

Ken considered the kid's attire, but he figured they could debrief in the time it took to get to the nearest coffee shop. "All right. But I don't have much time."

Belliveau grinned happy as a schoolboy. "Where to?"

"There's a café at the bottom of the stairs, right across from City Hall."

"Sounds good."

They started walking across the plaza, headed towards a staircase that led down to street level of a major throughfare. A brisk wind blew through the plaza, and Ken really wasn't able to use the walk as an opportunity to discuss the events in court.

He just told Belliveau that he wanted to break away from the courthouse to avoid giving the defense an opportunity to restart discussions with the trial judge. As an older lawyer, Boyle had some clout and wouldn't shy away from asking for a moment to add to his argument on the record. Leaving before he could do so was the best option.

At the bottom of the steps, Ken approached a side entrance to a coffee shop. He held the door for Belliveau to enter.

The place was a local chain that tried to present like an upscale café, but the repurposed tables were shellacked with a glossy finish to provide protection for high levels of foot traffic. The coffee was often lukewarm, and the pastries dried out. It really wasn't the gourmet coffee shop and bakery it claimed to be.

They ordered coffees, then found a table off to the side.

Ken explained the process for a motion to dismiss, compared to dismissals sought though summary judgment after a case underwent some discovery. Belliveau had a lot of questions about the rationale for opposing counsel's tactics.

Rather than speculate with the client about the other side's motives, he just responded, "They took their best shot at getting an early dismissal."

"But that's good for us?" Belliveau said. "The way the judge ruled."

"Sure."

"You don't sound too happy. Didn't we just get a big win in there."

Ken shrugged. "We got a favorable ruling. Not all judges would have gone that way. But you can expect they'll come back with further reasons for seeking dismissal of our case."

Belliveau looked concerned. "Even after what happened in there."

"Unfortunately, a lawyer like that won't necessarily abide by that decision. He may come up with new reasons for seeking dismissal, or he'll reshape what he already argued."

"Won't the judge get mad if he comes back with the same arguments?"

"Depends," Ken said. "It could be an entirely new judge by the time it gets to trial. Sometimes there's a slightly different spin, even the same judge might let him get away with it."

"That's not fair."

"It really depends on how you look at it. The judge spanked him for bringing that motion early. If he comes up with something new during discovery, she might think it fair to give him another shot."

"What could he come up with?"

"Beats me."

"So, what's next?"

"We'll undergo some discovery and try to get the matter scheduled for trial as quickly as possible."

"Why is that?"

"Look at what they came up with in the last couple of weeks. Less time for them to dig around, the better."

"Understood," Belliveau said, cracking a smile. "I'm happy to get paid sooner rather than later."

Ken thought about explaining that a verdict is only half the battle. Oftentimes in cases like this, the defendants file an appeal. Then you can undergo a collections process if they don't pony up and pay the judgment. He decided to have that discussion another day.

"What's going on with the firearm's case?" Belliveau said.

Ken felt his blood begin to boil.

"What's wrong?" asked Belliveau.

"A couple of things," Ken said, curtly. "First, you haven't gotten me the documents that you promised. I can't go forward with drafting a complaint without them."

"Okay. I'll get them to you. And?"

"And, you just paid the retainer a week ago."

"Figured you might have gotten started on it. That's all."

Ken couldn't believe what he was hearing. It wasn't uncommon for clients to think that they had the only case. They didn't know what else a lawyer was juggling. But this was ridiculous. The kid knew that Ken had spent an enormous amount of time over the last week gathering support for the motion to dismiss hearing in Belliveau's case.

"Well, I've expended a lot of time preparing for a motion to dismiss in another matter."

"I hear you on that," Belliveau said, chuckling at the comment.

A moment later, Belliveau's phone buzzed. He stepped off to the side and got into a heated argument with the girl he was seeing. Ken watched as the tendons in the kid's neck tightened into cables. Belliveau grinded his teeth whenever she spoke. It was like he could barely hold himself back while waiting for his opportunity to speak.

Belliveau didn't talk respectfully. He was railing off at her right in the coffee shop.

Ken looked around. There were a few lawyers present, and he regretted agreeing to this meeting.

He then considered whether he should dump the case and the client.

Belliveau ended the call and looked over at Ken. It almost seemed as though Belliveau had read Ken's mind. Agitation from the argument with his girlfriend shifted into a rage, which percolated under the surface of the young man's visage.

PART FOUR

DISCOVERY

THIRTY-TWO

THE HOLIDAYS came around and Ken was able to get an early trial date for Judge Wexler's DUI case. The parties had propounded discovery in Belliveau's police misconduct matter, and the client had yet to provide the invoices and paperwork needed for the firearms matter.

The insurance defense lawyers from Boyle's office had provided minimal discovery. It wasn't much more than a defendant would get in a criminal case: a police report, a few affidavits, and police logs.

Ken's trip to the precinct to complete the police report on his damaged car had been met with a lot of onlookers and heckling. His routine handling of a few matters hadn't been viewed by the police as a lawyer just doing his job. They held a grudge and he worried just how far they would go. Their conduct made him wonder if Judge Wexler had been set up.

The insurance company determined that Ken's Volkswagen was a total loss.

He settled up with them and held off buying a new car, relying upon public transportation instead. But it was only a matter of time when a car would be needed to go to court or a deposition outside the city.

After a long paperwork day in the office, Ken left to meet Alyson at the fancy restaurant diagonal from his office. He stepped outside into a winter wonderland, as snow cascaded and danced in the gusts of wind blowing through the financial district.

Most of the buildings were shut down and people had gone

home for the night. Downtown tended to become desolate around the holidays, except for holiday office parties at the various restaurants. The night was dark, aside from the dim glow of streetlights.

He trucked across State Street and entered the restaurant. Ken felt an immediate relief from the elements, despite having only been outside for a few minutes.

Scanning the place, he found Alyson seated at the bar. She was flanked by a few colleagues from her office. He headed over to meet her and greeted the prosecutors kindly. They nodded their heads and said a friendly hello. But none of them seemed sincere.

He wasn't one of them anymore. Mickey had given him another bonus equal to their annual pay. Ken was considering buying a condominium and he'd looked at a used Porsche.

There was a financial divide that separated them.

Alyson gave him a peck on the cheek.

Ken wasn't sure whether he should slip out of his overcoat and take a seat at the bar, or whether they would grab a table. She didn't provide him with any cues.

"Do you want to stay here?" Ken asked. "Or do you want me to get us a table?"

"A table!" one of the prosecutors said.

"Who can afford to actually eat *here*?" another chimed in.

The third said, "We just grab a drink and nurse it, pretending to fit in here."

They all laughed, but Ken didn't think it was funny.

Another difference aside from the pay, he was putting in longer hours. Much longer. Lawyers working at the D.A.'s Office tended to leave at 5:00 PM, unless they had a really big trial going on. Ken was often leaving at 11:00 PM.

There was a great more deal of stress in private practice, too. Courts are lenient with busy prosecutors when it came to deadlines. Not so much for criminal defense lawyers. The civil cases dealt with large sums of money, and the criminal matters often had the potential of the client being incarcerated.

"You're all free to switch over to private practice any time you want," Ken said, grinning.

They broke into laughter. "Not on your life," a couple of them said.

"Every time you set a client loose, we have to be around for the next time he gets arrested," another said.

They kept it up for a few more minutes, until Ken turned away to order a drink.

Alyson seemed to find the banter amusing. She sat there with a sly grin, as though enjoying the needling they were giving Ken. He didn't particularly find them offensive, but the joking was immature and got old quickly.

He ordered a gin and tonic. By the time the bartender brought over Ken's drink, the crew had finished their cocktails.

"We'll leave you two alone," one of them said.

Then, the trio paid their tab and sauntered out the door.

"A fun crew," Ken said.

"They're not that bad. Besides, the boss has to hold court every now and then."

It hadn't registered with Ken when he walked through the door that they all worked under her now. The scene just appeared to be the commonplace situation where a few guys go out with the attractive girl in the office and try to act witty.

He took a sip of his drink. "I guess so."

"You did the same when you were in my shoes."

"Sure. But I typically did it after a good development broke."

"How do you know we don't have a good development?"

Ken shrugged. "I don't. It's not like we can talk about work anymore."

"Whose fault is that?" she griped.

He didn't know what to say. Ken was taken aback by her comment, but he also felt like he was the cause of the issue. There was so much he wanted to tell her about the pitfalls of private practice.

"Do you want to order dinner?" he said, changing the subject.

Alyson nodded. She looked a little embarrassed about her

outburst.

The bartender came over and they put in their orders.

When he turned away, Alyson reached into a pocket of her coat draped over the barstool. "I wanted to wait to give you this," she said, sliding a small, giftwrapped present onto the bar.

"Alyson," Ken said, smiling. "It's not Christmas yet."

"I know," she said. "I was hoping it might help smooth things over."

Ken took the present and quickly tore it open. There was something in a plastic case. It was some type of electronic gadget. He perused it, confused.

"It's an iPhone," Alyson offered.

Ken chuckled. "I figured it was something like that. This is really great."

Alyson leaned over and gave him a quick kiss.

"Thanks," he said, staring at the gift with pleasure.

THIRTY-THREE

KEN sat in a conference room across town, while Robert Boyle took a routine deposition in Belliveau's police misconduct case. Boyle wore a white dress shirt with the sleeves rolled up, along with a blue and maroon rep tie.

Snow whisked by the window that overlooked a channel separating South Boston from the rest of the city.

Boyle's firm was one of the first law firms to move into the lower rental market of South Boston. Their office was housed in an old mill building, while the rest of the firms relocated into fancy new office buildings with glass walls and views of Boston Harbor.

The defense had quickly noticed the deposition of Belliveau's aunt, likely thinking she represented a weak link in the plaintiff's case.

She was an elderly woman with a head full of thick, gray hair. Her neck was fleshy and gave her the appearance of a bulldog. The weight carried into her thick arms and chest, which stretched the fabric of her flower print shirt.

Ken sat a couple chairs down from the witness and Boyle sat across from her. The stenographer was at the head of the table. Trevor Belliveau sat next to Ken, and Boyle's associates were at the far end of the table taking notes.

The deposition wasn't going very well for the defense.

They had already deposed Trevor Belliveau and didn't get anything of value from that deposition. By the end, he was showboating and mocking some of their questions.

"Does your nephew live in your house, Ms. Belliveau?" Boyle

asked, flipping a page on his notepad, as if ready to take down a critical point.

"Yes, he most certainly does."

"How do you know this?" Boyle asked.

"How do I know that someone is living in my own house?" she said.

"Yes, that is the question."

"Well, it's an odd question. How do you know if someone's living in your house?"

Boyle cracked a grin, like he was amused by her comment. "Ma'am, I'm afraid that I have to ask the questions here."

Ms. Belliveau looked at the lawyer and considered her response. "He was breaking up with his wife and asked if he could stay with me. That was almost two years ago. He stays in the second-floor unit because I don't like living up there. I've got arthritis…"

"But how do you know that he actually stays up there?"

"Well, I can hear him walking around," she said.

Ms. Belliveau laughed at the simplicity of her answer and everyone in the room chuckled.

"How often do you hear him walking around up there?"

"Almost every night. And about every morning."

"Really?" Boyle sounded doubtful.

"Well, there are some mornings that I get up early and go out shopping, so I don't usually hear him on those mornings."

"You say that he lives there," Boyle continued. "But he doesn't pay rent, correct?"

"He doesn't pay rent. But he buys my groceries at times, and he pays the utilities."

"You could rent the unit upstairs," Boyle said, "for more than the cost of groceries and utilities."

"Mister, have you been to a grocery store lately?"

Boyle looked perturbed.

"I'm sorry," she said. "You ask the questions."

"That's right."

"I could probably rent it for more. But I don't want some bum living in my house when I could have little Trevor staying there. He's actually a big help. He cuts the grass and lately he's been shoveling. He brings in the groceries. Clears the snow off my car. You've got him all wrong. He's a decent young man."

"I'm sure you feel that way. But doesn't he live with his girlfriend?"

"Girlfriend?" Ms. Belliveau looked bewildered. She glanced around the table as if seeking an answer to a question.

"Yes. Doesn't he actually live with his girlfriend?"

She laughed. "I'm afraid that I don't know about any girlfriend."

Then, she looked at Trevor Belliveau with an admonishing stare, like he'd left her out of an important detail in his life.

He shrugged and raised his hands, like he didn't know what the lawyer was talking about.

She nodded, as though she had just concluded that Boyle was a fool.

"What about the stuff that you keep in the basement?" Boyle asked.

"Sure. What about it?"

"Do you keep your possessions separated from your nephew's belongings?"

"Pretty much."

"But not entirely?"

"I guess you can say that. It's not like there's separate rooms down there."

Boyle cracked a grin, pleased with himself. "Well, I guess that about wraps things up," he said. "You are free to go."

Boyle stood up, which was meant to encourage the witness to get up and leave.

Ms. Belliveau sat there looking confused.

Ken turned to her. "That's okay, Ms. Belliveau. I have just a few questions for you."

She nodded. "You go right ahead."

Boyle sat back down, peeved that his tactic hadn't worked.

"There is an area with a piece of carpet on the floor, correct?"

Ken asked.

"Yes."

"Does your nephew keep his belongings on that carpet?"

"Objection to form!" Boyle said.

Ms. Belliveau looked at Boyle, wondering what to do.

"That's okay," Ken said. "You can answer."

"Yes. That's his carpet, too."

Trevor laughed.

"Do you keep your possessions on that carpet?"

"Well, I try not to... because that's his stuff on it."

"So, if you put anything on the carpeted area, is it just temporarily?"

"Objection," Boyle said. "The lawyer is testifying."

Ms. Belliveau looked around again, wondering what Boyle's objections were about.

"That's okay," Ken said, grinning. "You can ignore him. I'm not paying attention to him."

"Let's see," Ms. Belliveau muttered. "Do I keep my things on Trevor's rug... I'd say that I don't. But I have put things over there. Stacked something on his stuff to get at some boxes. I don't always put the things I've moved back right away."

"But you consider the carpeted area as a place for his stuff?"

She nodded.

"You have to answer verbally."

"I do. Yes."

"Now, there's a storage locker down in the basement..."

"Yes. That was my husband's."

Boyle sat back and grinned like a Cheshire cat. He acted like he'd just hit a home run.

"Can I take a quick break to use the restroom?" Ms. Belliveau said.

"Sure you can," Boyle said.

Everyone stood up and filed out of the conference room.

Boyle and his associates headed off to a nearby office to regroup and strategize next steps. Ms. Belliveau trundled down to the restroom and the stenographer followed her.

Trevor Belliveau pulled Ken into a jog in the hallway. He was teeming with anger. "Why did you go and ask a question like that?"

"Better to ask it now than to learn about it at trial."

"They were going to stop asking questions," Belliveau carped. "It never would have come out."

"It would have come out at trial, and we wouldn't know how to address it."

"Still, you shouldn't have asked any questions."

Ken considered the comment. Clients often want a case to go as long as they can keep it alive, while lawyers on a contingency fee prefer to know early if the case will ultimately fail, so they don't invest more time than necessary into it.

Discovery in contingency fee cases often involves a plaintiff's lawyer assessing his own case.

"Let's just figure out a way to fix this," Ken said.

"Sure. Here's the deal…"

***

AFTER the break, the witness settled back into her chair and Ken was ready to ask her more questions.

Just as he was about to speak, Boyle interrupted. "Excuse me," Boyle said. "Did you at any time during the break talk with Mr. Dwyer or your nephew?"

"I said hello to Trevor when I walked past him in the hallway on my way back from the ladies room."

"Anything else?" Boyle asked.

"You've got to be kidding me," Ken said.

"Well, counselor," Boyle said, patronizingly. "I've got a right to know."

"You're interrupting my questioning. You may have a right to know, but not while I have the floor. Now keep quiet, or I'm going to the judge."

Boyle sat back in his seat, miffed. He waved for Ken to proceed. "I've got the answer. So, there's no use wasting time with this debate."

"Are you done talking?" Ken barked.

"Yes. Please proceed."

Lawyers like Boyle are accustomed to getting their way. They interrupt when they are supposed to keep quiet as a means of establishing control. Ken knew that he had to jab the guy, or it wouldn't stop for the rest of the case.

"Ms. Belliveau," Ken said, kindly. "Tell us what happened to the storage locker after your husband died."

"He gave it to Trevor."

"Okay."

"We couldn't have kids," she said. "So, Trevor was like a son to him. When my husband died, he left several possessions to Trevor in his will."

"Sure."

Trevor Belliveau looked across the table at Boyle and sneered at the defense lawyer.

"What happed to the storage locker after it was given to Trevor?"

"He took it when he got married."

"Do you know what happened after that?"

"He brought it back to my house when he moved in."

"Did you ever use the storage locker?"

"Why would I need that old thing?" Ms. Belliveau said, sarcastically.

"Please answer the question."

"No."

"Thank you."

"I don't have any tools," she continued, "or any jars full of nuts and bolts."

"Thank you. That will be all."

Boyle resumed examining the witness. He tried to shake her loose from the damming testimony, but he didn't get anywhere. He threw his pen down on his notepad at the end of the day, likely realizing the case didn't have support for a dismissal on summary judgment.

The case had sufficient evidence to get to trial. Yet, the defendants were reluctant to make a settlement offer. It appeared like they planned to make Ken earn the result.

THIRTY-FOUR

THE NEXT WEEK, Ken found himself back in the Boston Municipal Courthouse in a packed courtroom, seated at the defense table while the prosecutor presented evidence against Judge Wexler. She appeared despondent.

Alyson did not attend the trial. She was first chairing a manslaughter case, so supervision of this matter was handed off to a less experienced lawyer. Courtney Richardson sat beside the young prosecutor, providing him with tips and direction. Ken had learned that the kid's name was Steve Fabinsky.

The place was crowded with the press, which clearly made Fabinsky nervous. He stuttered at times and constantly tripped over himself.

Ken found himself objecting to many questions and threw Fabinsky off his game.

Judge Honeycutt sat on the bench overseeing the trial.

The prosecution would have been better off with Richardson taking the lead. Ken had worked with her before leaving the D.A.'s Office. She was a natural born trial lawyer and handled herself well on the fly. With flowing blonde hair, an athletic build, and impeccable dress, Richardson exuded the type of credibility that comes with the position of prosecutor. She could easily be handling press conferences for the evening news.

After receiving the police report in discovery before trial, Ken had strategized a pathway forward. He hoped that the testimony of the arresting officer would fold in with his plans.

Despite a lackluster performance, Fabinsky had presented enough evidence to support an arrest through the police officer's testimony.

Ken stood up and walked into the well of the courtroom. "Officer Doyle, you testified on direct examination that you conducted the so-called wand test on the defendant, correct?"

"Yes." The officer sat in the witness box with a veneer woodgrain finish.

"The police report noted your findings, right?" Ken said.

"Sure did." The officer cracked an arrogant grin. He looked around the courtroom to check to see if anyone was amused by his antics.

Only a few people snickered. Everyone else had stone faces.

"You had the defendant undergo a heel-to-toe walk, too?"

"Yes. That's pretty standard."

"The police report noted your findings?"

"It did." The officer grinned at the softball questioning. He'd likely testified a hundred times.

"You didn't write the report at the scene?" Ken asked.

"No. It would have been written back at the station."

Ken walked over to his table and grabbed the police report. "When did you write this report?" he said, waving it.

"I don't recall."

"May I approach the witness to refresh his recollection, Your Honor?"

"You may," Judge Honeycutt said.

Ken walked past the jury box and a few jurors glanced at the document in Ken's hand, as if curious about what he was going to do next.

Placing the report in front of the witness, Ken asked, "Does that refresh your memory as to when the report was written?"

The witness perused the document, then he set it down. "Yes, it does."

Ken retrieved the police report. "When was it written?"

"Uh, it was uh, written three days after the arrest," the cop said, sheepishly.

"Why was this report," Ken said, holding it up, "written three days after the arrest?"

"Sir, well… uh," the cop mumbled. "I think I got off shift late that night, and I didn't get to it. Then, I had a couple days off, so I did it when I reported back to duty."

"Three days after the arrest?" Ken said.

"Yes."

"Did you memorize the results of the wand test?"

"Sir?"

"Where did you get the information about the field tests to put in your report?"

"I keep a notebook."

"You keep a notebook?"

"Sure." The cop straightened up, regaining confidence. "I write down the test results in a notebook. Then I record them on the police report later."

"This wasn't your only traffic stop that night?"

"No." The officer chuckled at the question.

"You worked late that night?"

"Apparently so."

"You undertook other field sobriety tests that night?"

"Uh, sure."

"How many?"

"I'm not sure," the officer said.

"More than three."

"Yes. It was a busy night."

"More than five?"

"Yes."

"More than ten?"

The officer shrugged. "Probably about eight to ten. Like I said, it was a busy night."

"How many traffic stop reports did you write, three days later, for the night of the defendant's arrest?" asked Ken.

The officer looked at Ken like a deer staring at headlights. The cop then looked over at the prosecution table for help. Fabinsky merely shrugged, like *you're on your own.*

"About half of them," the cop finally said.

"Half?"

"About that, yes."

"Half the reports from the night of the defendant's arrest were written three days after her arrest, correct?"

"I believe that I said that, yes."

"You probably needed your notebook to figure out what test results went with each suspect, right?" Ken said.

The officer smiled proudly. "Yes. It comes in handy."

"Could you have made a mistake when transposing the information from the notebook to the police reports for your various traffic stops?"

"I try to be careful."

"You try to be careful?"

"Certainly."

"So, there is some potential for error?" Ken said.

"If you were not careful, there could be a potential for error." The cop grinned. "That's why I *always* try to be careful."

"Do you have your notebook with you?"

The officer looked bewildered. "Uh, no. I don't."

"You relied upon it when you completed your report, right?"

"Yes, but—"

"And you didn't bring it to court?"

"No. Nobody has ever asked for it before..."

Ken walked over to the defense table and shoved the report into a manilla folder. Then, he picked up the folder and waved it back and forth. "Your notebook wasn't produced in this matter, right?"

"Well, uh... the prosecutor handles that."

"May I approach, Your Honor?"

"You may." Judge Honeycutt seemed to have a keen interest in what happened next.

"I'll represent to you that this is the complete discovery file that we received from the prosecution," Ken said, placing the folder on the edge of the witness box.

Fabinsky stood up. "Objection, Your Honor." It came out sounding nasally.

"Basis?" Judge Honeycutt asked.

"Well, he didn't show it to me."

Judge Honeycutt looked at Ken.

"Your Honor, it's his own file," Ken said, flatly. "He should know what's in there."

"Upon representation of counsel, the objection is overruled." She looked at Ken. "After you show it to the witness, you need to show it to opposing counsel."

"Sure, Your Honor."

The officer looked up at Ken like a steer headed to slaughter.

"Do you see a copy of your notebook in that file?"

The officer flipped through the materials in the folder. "No, sir. I don't."

"Thank you." Ken took the folder and started for the prosecution table.

"Nobody asked for it," the cop blurted. "No one's ever asked!"

Ken paused in the well of the courtroom. He half turned to the witness. "Your Honor, we move to strike," Ken said. "There wasn't a question pending."

"Granted." She looked at the jury. "You will disregard the witness's last comment."

Judge Wexler was following along intently, but she looked concerned and Ken worried that any dismay would send the wrong message to the jury.

Stepping over to the prosecution table, Ken handed the manilla folder to Fabinsky. The young lawyer nervously looked through it. He nodded, as if confirming the notebook wasn't in there. Then he handed the folder back to Ken.

Like he didn't already know the notebook wasn't in there, Ken thought.

"The defense moves to strike the officer's testimony relative to his field test results being logged into a notebook that was not produced," Ken said.

"The court will reserve ruling on that request," the judge said. "Continue."

Judge Wexler appeared relieved for the first time since the trial started.

Ken then began to cross-examine the police officer on the manner in which he undertook the heel-to-toe walk. The officer divulged that the defendant had informed him she'd recently undergone knee replacement surgery. He stated that he had considered the impact of the surgery when administering and evaluating the test, as well as the impact of her age and weight and lack of recent physical fitness training.

"Do you have any education in medicine?" Ken asked.

"No."

"What about in physical therapy?"

"None."

"What is your educational background?"

"I have an associate's degree in criminal justice from Bunker Hill Community College."

"What about your work experience?"

"As I said on direct, I was an MP in the Army for four years. Then I've been a police officer for the last ten years."

"Nothing else?"

"A few odd jobs in high school."

"None in the medical field?"

"That's right."

Ken walked behind his table. "The defense moves to strike the witness's testimony on the heel-to-toe walk test results."

"Reserved," Judge Honeycutt said. "Anything else?"

"I've concluded my examination of this witness for now, Your Honor."

"Very well," she replied.

Ken sat down.

"Any redirect?" the judge asked Fabinsky.

"Just a few questions," he said, standing up.

The redirect questioning didn't cure any of the issues Ken had raised during his cross-examination. When Fabinsky finished his redirect, Ken didn't have any follow up questions.

"Any further witnesses," Judge Honeycutt asked Fabinsky.

"No, Your Honor," he replied. "The prosecution rests."

She looked at Ken. "Mr. Dwyer, do you have something for

me?"

Ken stood up, thinking it was a good sign that the judge asked him before he even raised the issue. "Can we approach, Your Honor?"

"You may."

Ken and the other two lawyers walked up to the bench for a sidebar.

"The defense moves for a directed verdict," Ken whispered so the jury couldn't hear.

"You'll need to state the basis on the record."

Ken nodded, then he quietly spoke. "First, there was a gap in time between the field tests and the writing of the report. The officer admitted that transposing the field test results from his notebook to the report has a potential for error. Coupled with this, there were several reports being written at the same time. The margin for error increased. The defense has the right to the notebook to ascertain whether a transposition error took place. But the trial already had started, and jeopardy has attached, and the prosecution never turned over the notebook."

"Anything else?"

"Second, the defendant had undergone surgery and the officer considered the impact of the surgery on his field test results. He does not have any medical training or experience, so he cannot possibly factor what impact her surgery had on her field test results. He's not an expert. His testimony and his conclusions are tantamount to an expert opinion. An expertise the witness simply does not have."

Judge Honeycutt looked at Fabinsky and Richardson. "Response."

"The primary source of the information is the officer, not the notebook," Fabinsky said.

The judge looked at him skeptically.

"Well, he's got some first-aid training from the Army."

The judge shook her head. She wasn't buying it. "You all may return to your seats."

After the judge shooshed the lawyers away, she addressed

everyone in the courtroom. "The defense has requested a motion for a directed verdict. Given the circumstances of the delay between the field tests and the writing of the report, along with the volume of reports written at the time, the court agrees with the defense that there was a chance of transposition errors. The court does not find that there were any errors. However, we simply do not know because the arresting officer's notebook was not produced, nor was it presented at trial."

She paused and looked from counsel table to counsel table.

"The court also finds that the arresting officer does not have the expertise to evaluate the impact of knee replacement surgery on the walking test of someone the defendant's age and stature."

Murmurs resounded throughout the gallery, as the audience registered what was coming.

"The court does not find any of these factors *alone* as controlling on any case going forward, but the combined factors found here result in this court dismissing this case with prejudice. The defendant shall report to the clerk and the parole officer in order to terminate the bail conditions. Afterwards, she is free to go. We remind her that the administrative suspension remains in place."

The courtroom erupted with commotion from the pews.

Judge Wexler spun Ken around and hugged him.

A wave of emotions crashed over him. Ken could hardly comprehend the result.

"This court is now in recess," Judge Honeycutt said, then she whisked away from the bench for the side door before the bailiff could instruct everyone to stand.

Ken took a deep breath, then he headed for the gate.

Birnbaum stood waiting for them with a wide grin. "Excellent job," he said, reaching to shake Ken's hand.

Ken shook the man's hand without consciously thinking about it. He was on autopilot.

Birnbaum took the lead and ushered Ken and Wexler from the courtroom.

"I've got to get some air," Ken said to them.

"Go," Birnbaum said. "We're going to duck into a meeting room. The three of us can catch up later."

Judge Wexler smiled. "Thank you, Kenny. Thank you for everything."

"It was my pleasure." He shook her hand, then he broke through the throng, as lightbulbs flashed, and reporters grabbed him trying to get a quote.

THIRTY-FIVE

RETURNING to the office, Ken ran into Mickey on the sidewalk near the Starbucks located at the corner of State Street and Merchants Way.

"Hey, how you doing?" Mickey said. "I thought you had the Wexler trial today."

"I did," Ken replied. "It's over."

"Over?" Mickey said, dumbfounded. "That soon?"

"Judge granted a directed verdict."

"You won? Holy shit."

Ken chuckled at the comment. He stood there for a moment wanting to unload his trial bag. After walking back from the BMC, he was ready to park himself in a chair.

"Hey, why don't you join me for a bite?" Mickey said after a moment. "On me."

"It's kind of early for dinner and late for lunch..." Ken said.

"But?" Mickey said, grinning.

"I haven't had lunch."

They both laughed. Then, they headed over to Mickey's favorite pub, and they found a high-top table by the window.

During the warmer months, the windows along Merchants Row were folded open. The place was typically jampacked all afternoon. Pedestrians traipsed past on their way to and from shopping in Faneuil Hall. But during the winter, few people walked by, and the restaurant was often barren.

It didn't take long for the server to approach.

Mickey ordered a Jameson's on the rocks. "Don't tell me," Mickey said to Ken. "You're going with a diet cola."

"Nope. A greasy burger and a Bass Ale."

Mickey grinned from ear to ear. "You're finally catching on."

They handed their menus over to Sandra and waited for her to return with the beverages.

Ken took a sip of his beer. It was cold and the glass was frosted over.

"How is it?" Mickey said.

"Perfect."

"Nothing like winning a high-profile case," Mickey said.

"True. Except losing one right afterward."

"What's on your mind?"

"The Belliveau case," Ken said.

"What about it?"

"The case is a tough one. We really don't have a lot to show for damages, and liability is questionable. A jury might think the police acted in good faith. Despite the law, they might give the cops a free pass. No harm, no foul."

The server brought over their burgers, then they dug in.

Mickey let him enjoy the meal for a bit. He seemed to ruminate over Ken's comments about the case. Clearly, the seasoned trial lawyer didn't find Ken's assessment off point, or he would have shot it down.

"Cases like this," Mickey said, pausing to sip his drink. "When you have cases like this, it comes down to credibility. You have to show the police are bad actors."

"How do I do that?"

"Two things," Mickey said. "You come up with a theory. And you hire a private investigator to dig up dirt on the key witness. Don't use anything from the PI during depositions. That would only inform them of your investigation and help them prepare for trial. Just onload with it at trial. Got it?"

"Yeah," Ken said. "But that was three or four things. Not two."

They got in a good laugh. Then Ken finished his meal and returned to the office. He spent the entire evening preparing for depositions in Belliveau's case.

THIRTY-SIX

NEXT MORNING, Ken woke early after a restless night. It was just a day of depositions, but he felt stress from having to perform live in front of people two days in a row.

After he got the coffee pot started, he flicked on the news. Then, he walked over to the door to his apartment, opened it, and bent down and grabbed the morning's paper.

The headline was surprising: Judge Avoids Jail Time on Technicality.

A picture of Judge Wexler walking out of court with a smile on her face was plastered to the front of the paper. There was a short write-up of the trial with a few comments about Ken. Much of the piece made the prosecution look foolish.

Alyson was smart to have avoided the trial. Ken wondered if she sensed that she was dodging a bullet. Like a savvy political animal, she had gotten in the press at the opportune time, and then stepped out of the picture at the time of the prosecution's demise. He wondered if she had better instincts than he'd ever realized. He also wondered how far her ambitions went.

Flipping to the continued section, Ken was shocked to see a half-page picture of him walking out of the courtroom.

The subheading read: Former Prosecutor Dazzles a Victory.

He'd started to read the article when the news station switched to another story. Ken and Judge Wexler's faces appeared in boxes on the screen. It must have been a slow news day, and so the judge's dismissal was circulating everywhere.

Glancing at the clock, Ken had to get ready for the depositions. He'd have to catch up on the news article and stories later.

Once he was showered and shaved and dressed in a decent suit, Ken headed out into the cold and caught the subway over to his office. He walked in and Belliveau was seated in a chair in the small reception area. The stenographer was already setting up in the conference room.

"I'll just be a moment," Ken said to Belliveau.

He headed back to his office and hung his overcoat on a hanger on the back of the door. Then he stepped over to Pat's workstation. "Anything new?" he said.

She smiled and shook her head. "Nope."

It was good news. Often, things had a way of blowing up right when a lawyer was heading into court or a deposition.

"Nice," Ken said, grinning.

He was feeling better already. In the zone.

Ken walked over and said hello to Belliveau. The kid finally wore a coat commensurate with the weather. It was a leather jacket with sherpa lining.

"Do you want me to take your coat?" Ken said.

Belliveau looked around, as though wondering where it would be stored.

"We have a closet back by Pat," Ken said. "Nothing will happen to it."

Belliveau reluctantly removed his jacket and handed it to Ken.

After Ken hung up the coat, he returned to reception.

The elevator dinged and the doors rattled open.

Boyle and a police officer stepped onto the floor. They appeared cold and projected an intimidating presence. Neither of them said a word at first.

"We'll be in here," Ken said, indicating to the conference room.

"I've been in there plenty of times," Boyle said.

"Can I get you anything to drink?" Ken asked. "Water, coffee?"

"No," Boyle said, answering for both of them. "We're fine."

"Are the others coming?" Ken said.

He had noticed the depositions of all three officers involved in the search to occur in the same day. There wasn't a lot of ground to cover, so he planned to plow through them rather quickly. Officer Berwick was scheduled first.

"We have everyone lined up to come over as needed," Boyle said, with a reassuring tone. "Officers can't come off the street and hang around for hours waiting to be deposed. They have more important things to do."

Ken didn't care for Boyle's tone, but he let the comment slide.

They all got set up in the conference room, with the stenographer seated at the head of the table. Her back was against the window overlooking State Street. Boyle directed Berwick to sit near the stenographer with the bookcase behind him. Then Boyle took a seat next to his client and fished out a notepad from his trial bag.

Ken sat across from the witness and Belliveau sat next to him.

Clients are typically busy with work and don't attend depositions of other parties or fact witnesses. Belliveau seemed to have all the time in the world, and it made Ken wonder whether the kid really was involved with a prescription drug ring.

Ken got the deposition underway, and the burly Boston police officer never broke from his stoic countenance. This caused Ken to keep the questioning tight to avoid allowing the witness opportunities to explain himself.

Once Berwick's deposition was concluded, the next Boston officer took about twenty minutes to arrive. Officer O'Rourke had testified at the motion to suppress hearing. He appeared with a similar demeanor to the first witness. Ken knew he wouldn't get anywhere with the witness, so he followed the same approach as he had taken with the first officer.

Boyle had set the order of witnesses based upon his representation of their ability to attend the depositions due to scheduling issues.

The third officer was Kyle Randle, a Lynn cop assigned to the task force. He showed up for his deposition a half hour after they had finished with the second witness. He appeared younger than the first two, and he wasn't as surly. Ken thought Randle looked nervous. So much so, that Ken figured Boyle had set the order of the depositions, so the weakest link went last. The other officers probably prepped him before Randle showed up.

Ken was glad that he hadn't revealed all his cards during the other two depositions.

The stenographer swore the witness under oath.

Ken asked some background questions and learned that Randle had gone to Westfield State College and had been on the force for about three years. The kid got comfortable, and his confidence seemed to grow as Ken went through the background information.

"Did you speak to the other two officers named as defendants in this case prior to your deposition?" Ken said.

Randle sat back and considered the question. "Yeah. I mean we work together. Of course I've spoken with them." The response sounded cocky.

Boyle smirked at the comment.

"Did you speak to them today?" Ken barked.

"Yes," Randle admitted.

"Did you speak to them after each of them was deposed?"

"Yes." Randle looked at the table.

"How long did the first discussion last?"

"About an hour."

"What did the two of you discuss?"

"Oh, you know. This and that."

"Like what?"

Boyle leaned forward. "Objection."

"Like what?" Ken insisted.

The witness sat there, nonresponsive.

"You are required to answer every question, unless your counsel specifically instructions you not to do so," Ken said. "Like what?"

"He just told me… you know?"

"No, I don't. That's why I'm asking the question."

"Well, he mostly just made fun of you," Randle said. "Poked at you a bit, saying that you really didn't have a case and all."

"He didn't tell you what questions were asked?"

"He might have?"

"Did he, or didn't he?" Ken pressed.

Randle looked at Boyle as if hoping the lawyer would run interference. Ken figured Boyle pulled stunts like this all the time, but he probably didn't get caught very often. Now, he had to sit there and take his medicine.

"I'm waiting," Ken said.

"Sure. He mentioned some questions."

"Which ones?"

"I honestly can't recall." This sounded truthful.

"What about the other officer? Did you speak with him?"

"Yes. It was pretty much the same thing, except that discussion was a lot shorter."

Ken went over the standard protocols for a search warrant, questioning Randle about his usual handling of a search.

"You agree it's best practice to obtain a search warrant before entering a house?" Ken said.

"Sure. But there are exceptions."

Randle spoke firmly and was clearly well prepared for this line of questioning. Boyle was so confident that he sat back and stopped taking notes. He almost seemed to lose interest in the deposition.

"Exigent circumstances?" Ken asked.

"Yes."

"But there weren't any exigent circumstances?" Ken said. "Were there?"

"Well, it depends on how you look at it," Randle said. "When you're investigating a serious crime with detrimental impacts on the public, everything is exigent."

"Not under the law."

"Objection," Boyle stammered. "Counsel is testifying."

"What was exigent, here?" asked Ken.

"Uh, I..."

"Why didn't you get a warrant?" Ken said, picking up the pace.

"Officer Berwick said we didn't need one."

"What's your understanding as to why one wasn't needed?" Ken said.

Ken was asking the questions rapid fire. Once an answer was given, he pressed with a new question. He leaned forward intently and spoke with a sharp tongue. This caused the witness to respond in kind without pausing and thinking about his answers.

"Figured we'd just get consent from the aunt. Maybe she was a nice lady and would let us look around?" Randle offered. His tone reflected he was hoping to convince Ken. It came across like begging for acceptance of the answer.

"Weren't you concerned about any evidence that was seized being tossed?" Ken said.

"I think we were more concerned about letting it sit," Randle blurted. He looked nervous as soon as the response came out, like he realized that he'd made a major misstep.

Let the evidence sit, Ken thought. *Let the contraband sit.*

"How well do you and the other two officers know each other?" Ken asked.

"I don't know them nearly as well as they know each other," Randle said calmly, like he was answering another softball question. "I mean they're both with the BPD, and I work in Lynn. Besides, the two of them have been living together since Berwick separated from his wife."

Ken sat back and decided to roll through the rest of the deposition like he had done with the first two officers. He was homing in on the approach for trial and didn't want to flag the theme he was thinking about using in the case.

When he concluded the deposition, Ken felt his confidence in proving liability shoot way up. He was pleased and turned to Belliveau. But the young man stared at him with ire in his eyes.

THIRTY-SEVEN

ONCE everyone filed out of the conference room, Belliveau stood up and paced around the small space, bunching his fists. He was furious.

Ken waited for Belliveau to speak to determine the reason for the anger.

"That's not how you ask questions," Belliveau said.

"What do you mean?" Ken said.

"You dig in, you pin them down. You *don't* talk to them nicely."

Ken had it with the jailhouse lawyering. He wondered where Belliveau got all his experience with deposition testimony. That morning, Ken was being featured in the press for pulling off an incredible trial result. Now, this kid was questioning him on basic legal skills.

Walking across the room, Ken gently closed the door.

Then he took a seat at the conference room table. "Please sit down."

Belliveau reluctantly took a seat across from Ken.

"We've got this matter on a fast track for trial. The deposition testimony that we got today was actually quite helpful."

"Helpful?" Belliveau repeated. "We didn't get squat from it?"

Ken tried to explain the theme he wanted to use in the case, but Belliveau wouldn't have it. "I think that's a lousy way to go."

"It's the best approach for a case like this."

"A case like this. A case like this!" Belliveau sat back and glared at him.

"I'm just trying to—"

"You have no idea how tired I am of you saying *a case like this!*"

"Listen, if you want to get another lawyer..."

"I want *you* to do *your* job!"

Ken hadn't found the initial outburst upsetting. But the allegation of him not doing his job was troubling when he'd expended evenings and weekends working on the case. He wanted to explode and punch the kid in the face.

"And another thing," Belliveau continued. "We need to file a motion of summary judgment."

"We can't do that," Ken snapped. "This case comes down to what a reasonable police officer would do under the circumstances. It will go to the jury to decide."

Belliveau shook his head, condescendingly. "No. I've read up on this."

Ken couldn't believe where this was going. He sat back and crossed his arms.

"If you have undisputed facts," Belliveau said. "Then they enter judgement as a matter of law."

"Except—"

"We have undisputed facts!" Belliveau yelled.

"You're shaky on the law. A jury gets to decide whether those facts represent a violation of your civil rights based upon—"

"You just don't want to do the work! It's not billed per hour."

Ken's blood boiled. "You listen here."

Belliveau reached into his pocket and fished out his cellphone. He set it on the table and started pressing buttons.

"Are you trying to record our discussion?" Ken demanded.

Belliveau just looked at him. Suddenly, the kid went from being irate to having a look of concern.

"You should know that recording a discussion is illegal. And I... do *not*... consent to being recorded."

"I'm not doing anything," Belliveau said. "Just checking my messages."

Then, he pressed a few more buttons and slid the phone back

into his pocket.

"Look, if you don't like how I do things..."

"What?" Belliveau said. "Are you going to tell me to get another lawyer?" A sinister grin spread across Belliveau's face, like he knew something, but he wasn't going to reveal it.

"I have ethical obligations and cannot file a motion that I think is meritless."

"Ethical obligations?" Belliveau said, scoffing at the comment.

Ken couldn't believe where this discussion had led.

Then Belliveau stood up. "I'll be right back."

He walked over and opened the conference room door. Then he retrieved a backpack from beneath the seat in reception, where he had been sitting when he had been waiting earlier.

Belliveau came back. He tossed a stack of documents on the conference room table.

"That's the stuff you wanted for the firearms case," Belliveau said. "I want you to get started on it. You've been sitting on the retainer forever."

The kid started for the door.

He stopped and turned around. "I just don't want my case to be handled half-assed."

Ken stood up. He was flabbergasted by the turn of events.

"No need to walk me out," Belliveau said.

Then, he headed down the corridor and fetched his coat. He walked back to the reception area, put on the jacket, slung the backpack over a shoulder, while ignoring Ken the entire time. When the elevator doors opened, he stepped inside.

Before the doors closed, Belliveau called out: "You're *my* lawyer."

THIRTY-EIGHT

THE ordeal with Belliveau from the night before weighed heavy on Ken's mind. He didn't sleep that night and longed to call Alyson and tell her about the situation. But he suffered through the night alone. Ken woke up in the morning not feeling any better.

When he got to the office, he asked Pat whether she had been disturbed by the discussion with Belliveau. She played the whole situation down. Pat merely commented that there had been some grumblings from the conference room.

He asked her if she had heard any shouting. Pat said that she wouldn't characterize it as shouting. Ken wasn't sure if she was giving him honest feedback, or if she was just telling him what he wanted to hear.

Maybe she was smarter and more experienced than he'd given her credit for. Her position would support him if Belliveau ever made a complaint to the bar.

Ken went to see Mickey later that morning and gave him the lowdown.

"Do you think you can win the case?" Mickey asked.

"Most likely," Ken answered in earnest.

"Then the solution is simple."

"It is?"

"Sure." Mickey said. "You just keep going and collect the fee."

"What about the firearms case?" Ken said.

"You can drop it as soon as you deposit the funds in our account from the police misconduct case." Mickey grinned.

"What if they appeal?" Ken said.

"You're stuck with Belliveau for a while."

Ken was left with a sinking feeling, like he wouldn't be able to unravel himself from the menacing kid. It was like Belliveau had him utterly ensnared.

THIRTY-NINE

KEN found work to keep himself busy for a few hours. By the time he stepped out of the office for lunch, he was feeling better.

The temperature had warmed up and the sun was shining bright. People had left their offices in droves. It created a milieu that caused Ken to feel more up-tempo. He decided to hoof it over to a sub shop over on Oliver Street.

After crossing the street near the Starbucks he heard someone calling. "Yeah you!"

Ken walked a little further. Then, he heard it again.

"Yeah you!" It was an authoritative voice.

Ken wondered what was going on, so he stopped and looked around.

Two uniformed police officers were headed in his direction. One of them was older and had his hand on the butt of his pistol. The other cop was younger and had a hand on his handcuff case.

"You've got to be kidding me," Ken said.

"Sir, please step over to the car," the older cop said.

"What's the meaning of this?" Ken insisted.

"Please step over to the car."

Ken walked over to the cruiser and the young officer shoved him over the hood of the car. Then, the cop proceeded to frisk him like a common criminal, right on State Street. They were in the middle of the financial district during the lunchtime rush.

People were all rubbernecking as they walked past.

"What's the meaning of this," Ken said, while pinned to the car.

"Caught you jaywalking."

Ken turned his head to look at the younger officer. "That's a violation. You can't place me under arrest for it."

"Listen to the bigshot lawyer," the older cop said. "Gets a little press and it goes straight to his head."

"The next press that I get is going to be for suing the two of you over a jaywalking fine," Ken said. "Let go of me."

The older cop nodded to the younger one. Then, the young officer eased up his grip and let Ken step back onto the sidewalk.

"What's the meaning of this?" Ken said. "I crossed right in front of the Starbucks. There's a crosswalk right there." He pointed to an area with crosswalk marks showing at the curb cuts on each side of the street, but the area in-between had totally faded away.

"That's not how I see it," the older cop said. "You cut across the street without entering the crosswalk. Ain't that how you see it, Tom?"

"Yup."

"This is crazy," Ken griped. "Look around. Nobody's using the crosswalk."

"We can't catch them all, counselor," the older cop said.

The younger officer wrote up a violation, then he tossed it at Ken. It bounced off Ken's midsection and landed on the sidewalk, quickly becoming soiled and wet.

"Good thing someone totaled your car," the older cop said. "Otherwise we might just pinch you for a DUI like your judge friend. And you wouldn't be able to represent yourself, like how you got the fancy judge's case tossed."

They climbed into the police car, and the older officer gave Ken a mock, friendly wave as they rolled off down the street.

***

KEN stepped into a nook jutting into the façade of the 75 State Street tower. He called Alyson and explained what had just happened.

"You need to call the dogs off," he said.

"I'll do what I can, Kenny," she said, earnestly. "But you know that no one can control these people. You seemed to have really pissed them off. All that press…"

She made it sound like it was all Ken's fault. "Anything else happens," he said after a moment. "I'm getting badge numbers and filing a lawsuit. I'll file a criminal complaint, too. They might need reminding that a private citizen can bring a criminal complaint for assault and battery."

"Will do," Alyson said. "And Kenny…"

"Yeah."

"Take care of yourself."

"Maybe I should drop the police misconduct case," he said.

"Really?" Alyson sounded happy.

"The client is driving me nuts. I don't know."

"Well, let's plan to get together soon." Alyson said. "Kenny, I do mean it. Take care of yourself."

"Okay," he said, ending the call.

Her last comment came across like something a person might say when they didn't expect to see another person for a long time. Ken got the feeling that it might signal the beginning of the end of their relationship if he didn't get away from civil rights and criminal defense cases. She was pro police, and he was becoming their arch enemy.

A few minutes later, Ken had resumed his walk towards the sub shop when he felt his phone vibrate.

He reached into his pocket, expecting Alyson had something more to say.

Instead, it was a text from an unknown number. He looked at it and an image appeared on the screen. It was him in a strip club with a topless dancer's arms wrapped around him. The picture didn't show anything graphic or depict him returning any interest; he wasn't kissing the girl. But it showed Ken in a compromised position.

A text read: *How would you like her to get this?*

Another appeared stating: *You're my lawyer.*

Somehow, the kid must had figured out a way to bug Ken's

phone. The timing of the text was too convenient. And now Ken knew why Belliveau had acted like he had something to hold over Ken's head.

PART FIVE

TRIAL

FORTY

TIME had passed and the holidays shifted into the dead of winter. Belliveau continued to hound Ken about both of his cases.

Ken had wanted to drop the man as a client, but he heeded Mickey's advice and tried to see the matters through. At least the police misconduct matter. Eventually, he met with Mickey at the local pub after work one night.

The place was packed, and they were lucky to find a spot at the bar.

Everyone around them was consumed with their discussions and talking so loudly that Ken and Mickey were able to talk about work issues without being overheard. Mickey drank his usual Jameson's on the rocks, while Ken nursed a Bass Ale.

Their discussions finally turned to Belliveau, and Ken revealed his concerns about the client.

After Ken told Mickey about his suspicions about Belliveau, the old trial lawyer looked at him skeptically. Mickey polished off his drink and ordered another without commenting on the information Ken had divulged.

"You don't believe that he drugged me," Ken said.

Mickey shrugged. "I don't know what to believe. Maybe he did, or maybe he didn't. Could be you had a couple too many, ended up at a strip club, and some clown thought it would be a hoot to slip the stiff in a suit a roofie."

"The guy is bad news," Ken said, pointing to accentuate his feelings.

"Sure. Most of them are, but that doesn't mean he drugged you."

"Come on," Ken said, spreading his hands.

"Even if he did, you couldn't prove it now," Mickey took a sip of his next drink.

Ken thought about the statement. Mickey was right. At this point, Ken could never prove it and making an accusation would likely just make him look foolish. Even Mickey was having a hard time swallowing it.

He hadn't reported it to the police or sought medical treatment because he'd been afraid of getting diagnosed with an illegal drug in his system. Now, Ken finally concluded that he'd made the right decision. There was no way to prove Belliveau had drugged him, not conclusively. Reporting the situation would have just made Ken look irresponsible in the least. At worst, he might be seen as a lawyer playing around with illegal drugs.

"You going to tell Alyson?" Mickey asked.

"Eventually."

"Probably should do so, sooner than later. You don't want a guy like that having any leverage over you."

"So, you think he's bad news?"

"Pretty much."

"Do you think he bugged my phone?"

Mickey looked at Ken and furrowed his eyebrows. "I don't know squat about them gadgets. But I do know a little about people. Trevor Belliveau is the controlling type. I could see him meddling with your phone to keep tabs on you."

Ken nodded, feeling validated.

"However, it's possible that you'd just gotten the text with the photo of the stripper around the time you happened to mention that you were thinking about dumping him as a client."

"So, it was just a coincidence."

"Could be," Mickey said. "But if I were you..."

"What?"

"I'd go trade that phone in for another one."

***

THE stack of documents that Belliveau had given Ken had sat in a pile on his credenza for months. Previously, the kid had called concerned the firearms case would miss a deadline. Belliveau was worried about the case missing the statute of limitations.

Ken couldn't see how a three-year limitations period could cause Belliveau to have such a concern when the divorce case had only been filed a couple years beforehand and the order about selling the firearms happened during the pendency of the divorce case. But he had gone ahead and filed the lawsuit to keep Belliveau from pestering him.

It didn't help. Belliveau was convinced they were under a deadline to produce documents. Ken figured the kid had read the rules from another jurisdiction, but he spent time reviewing the firearms documents when he should have been working on the police misconduct matter.

Although he noticed some peculiarities with the dates on the invoices and some of the items that had been purchased, Ken found that no deadlines were in jeopardy. In order to quiet Belliveau down, he instructed an associate that Mickey had recently hired to produce the documents to opposing counsel.

Ken then turned back to preparing for trial.

The new associate they hired was Joey Argenziano. He had recently graduated from Syracuse University Law School and had done some excellent legal research to help with the police misconduct case.

FORTY-ONE

KEN met with Belliveau in the conference room late one night after everyone had cleared out for the day. The police misconduct matter was swiftly approaching trial. The meeting was scheduled as a preparation session to get Belliveau ready for trial testimony.

Prior to the meeting, Ken had sent Belliveau his deposition transcript and told the kid to read through it prior to the meeting. Belliveau showed up to the meeting without the transcript and he hadn't read any of it.

Ken tried to go over Belliveau's testimony, but the kid merely wanted to strategize about the case. Belliveau kept asking about Ken's opening statement, what exhibits would be entered into evidence, and what the lawyer would ask the police officers when they testified. At times, Belliveau would suggest taking more depositions, even though discovery had closed. He kept asking if it was too late to file a motion for summary judgment.

All of this was repetitive discussions they'd had previously.

Throughout the meeting, Ken kept steering the discussion back to Belliveau's testimony.

"Look!" Ken said, finally growing tired of the nonsense.

Belliveau sat back in his chair, apparently surprised and taken aback by the outburst.

"You need to understand that you have a small role in this case," Ken snapped. "All you have to do is sit at counsel table and act calm and try to appear as likeable as possible. You don't frown at responses from the officers, and you don't start yacking in my ear about objecting or what to ask them. You put any comments down on a notepad. You got all that?"

"Okay..." Belliveau looked at him sheepishly.

"One thing you need to understand, your role in the case is to testify," Ken said. "You are a single witness. Everything else is up to me. Opening and closing statements. Examining the police officers, your aunt, selection of exhibits. None of that is your concern at this point."

"I'm just trying to make sure the case is handled properly," Belliveau said.

"That would be fine," Ken said. "Except, we've covered all this before. Many times. And now we're getting close to trial, and I don't have time for this."

"Well, as the client, I have a right—"

"A right!" Ken shot from his chair, and it rolled into the wall with a crash.

"Yeah," Belliveau, said smugly. But he looked scared.

"You don't like it, find another lawyer."

Belliveau sneered confidently. "I thought we'd already covered this."

He's talking about the stripper, Ken thought.

"You listen to me," Ken said, pointing. "And you listen good. Nobody bribes or coercers me. Nobody! You got that?"

Belliveau leaned back and smirked. "Sure. I have it, *Ken.*"

"Just try something. You'll find out..."

"Find out what, Ken?"

Ken wondered if the kid had turned on his phone. *Maybe the kid was recording this?*

"Just try me," Ken said, staring intently at the kid.

Physically fit and combat infantry experience likely made Ken appear dangerous to Belliveau in the small conference room, alone, late in the evening.

The foreboding presence caused the young man's smirk to slip away.

Belliveau stood up. "We should probably call it a night."

The kid packed up his stuff and slinked out of the conference room without saying another word. Ken heard the elevator ding

and when the doors rattled shut, he let out a sigh of relief.
This case can't end soon enough.

FORTY-TWO

LATER, the amount of work Ken could accomplish for the day expired, after he'd grown weary from fatigue. The meeting with Belliveau had taken much longer than he'd anticipated. It resulted in him working later to make up for the lost time.

He shut down the office and stepped out into the chilly night.

Spring wasn't far away, and the day had begun unseasonably warm. Ken had only worn a suit to work. Now, he wished that he'd opted for his short, tan trench coat. An extra layer of warmth could go a long way.

Ken had settled up with the insurance company after the adjuster had determined his Volkswagen was a total loss. He hadn't purchased a new car and was stuck taking public transportation. It was a desolate night and there wasn't a soul in sight.

Traipsing along the sidewalk, he shivered from the cold and picked up his pace. Ken started to cross Merchants Row when a car rolled up beside him.

Ken immediately recognized that it was a police car. He thought it was going to drive past, but then it halted beside him.

Glancing at the car, Ken recognized the person sitting in the passenger seat. It was the crass police officer that had taken the call for his hit-and-run. The window was down. Ken wondered if the guy had noticed him and had an update about the incident.

"Hey, counselor," the cop said.

"What can I do for you?" Ken replied.

"Just living the dream."

"Well, if you don't have any news for me," Ken said. "I'm

going to be on my way. It's kind of cold out here for small talk."

The cop flashed a knowing grin. "Perhaps you should move it along, then."

Ken resumed his trek towards the entrance to the subway, located near City Hall Plaza. He walked a block and waited for the light at Congress Street.

Looking back, the cruiser that had pulled up beside him remained parked at the entrance to Merchants Row. It was an odd place to stop. Ken thought the officers were arrogant, but then he considered nobody would be driving through there at this time of night.

A dark car rolled past the cruiser. It looked like an unmarked car.

The light turned and Ken started to cross the street.

Just as he entered the intersection, the dark car abruptly turned onto Congress Street and accelerated. It headed directly for Ken.

He bolted and the front of the car whisked past him.

The back end swung around, and tires skidded on the pavement.

A thump resounded as the quarter panel struck his legs.

The blow hurled Ken into the air and landed face first on the frigid pavement. The impacted jolted him, and everything was blurry. He heard the car tear off down the street. Dazed, he gathered himself and slowly rose to his feet.

His suit was torn at the knees. Ken felt stinging pain from his abrasions.

The cruiser rolled up next to him, and the gruff cop looked out the window and cracked a devious smile.

"Aren't you going after that guy?" Ken said.

"We can't catch them all."

"You're not even going to try."

"Best you watch out for those hit-and runs," the cop said, laughing. "You seem to have a lot of trouble with them."

"It was one our yours..."

"Who knows," the cop shrugged. "We'll be sure to put it in a report. Then we'll make sure to file it away somewhere."

Ken frowned. "Get the hell outta here."

"Will do."

Ken continued crossing the street and the cruiser rolled past.

"Maybe you should drop that case," the cop said.

Then, the car window was slowly raised, and the police car sped off down the street.

Ken stepped onto the sidewalk across the street, feeling safer to be on surer ground. He couldn't believe what had happened. There wasn't any doubt the police were sending him a message to drop the case. It made him think his theory was right on track.

He'd only walked a few feet when he heard brakes screech behind him.

Turning, he expected to find more cops out to harass him.

Instead, a dilapidated white van had rolled up behind him. The cargo door slid open, and a few thugs jumped from the van. They had an eastern European look to them. Greasy longer hair, black nose rings, tattoos on their necks.

The assailants wore jeans and black boots. Heavy dark coats completed their ensembles.

Ken wasn't going to wait for an introduction.

He turned and bolted up the sidewalk.

Another white van sped along the roadway and popped onto the sidewalk at a curb cut used by public works trucks.

Ken halted in his tracks. He considered fleeing through the plaza of 64 State Street, which ran between the office building and a few older buildings.

Just as he'd caught his breath and was ready to run, the passenger door to the other van opened. An older man with a short, receding hairline alighted from the vehicle. He shook his head, as if to suggest that no harm would come to Ken.

This man didn't wear a coat like the others. He was dressed in a long-sleeved undershirt. Wintry weather didn't seem to bother him.

He smiled, condescendingly.

As men from the other van rushed up behind Ken, the leader

slowly approached from the other direction. He seemed amused.

"Come now," the man said.

Ken looked at the man askance.

"Do you really think we intend to hurt you?"

"I don't know what you plan."

"If we wanted to hurt you, you'd be dead already."

"So, what do you want then?" Ken demanded.

"This is no different than the message your police friends sent," the gangster said. "Only ours is the opposite. And it's more potent."

"What do you want?"

"I want you to continue with the case. I've got sort of a wager on the case. Or maybe you Americans might consider it like a second position on a mortgage."

Belliveau owes him money, Ken thought.

The man smiled. "You've got it. I knew you were smart. Lawyer man."

"How much you got into it?" Ken asked.

"Fifty thousand."

"That might be more than the case is worth."

"Well, then I suggest you do a fantastic job." The man grinned.

The thugs piled back into the vans and tore off down the roadway, leaving Ken alone to ponder the predicament he'd gotten himself into with this case.

FORTY-THREE

STANDING in front of the jury during his opening statement, Ken focused on what the evidence would show. He explained the police hadn't found any drugs, and they had only seized legally owned tools, located in a storage locker owned and controlled by the plaintiff.

He hit upon these points first, so the jury didn't discount Belliveau's rights due to allegations of him being involved with illegal drugs.

Then, he followed up with the standard practice to obtain a warrant, and that warrantless searches should be used only in exigent circumstances, and there were none here. Many of the jurors followed along, but a few seemed disinterested.

They probably wondered how Belliveau suffered any actual harm.

Boyle's opening focused on the officers acting like any reasonable officer would act. He painted the picture of Belliveau being a dangerous person involved in an underground trade that was detrimental to the public. He too seemed to pick up on the disinterested jurors and put it out there. "Where's the harm?" he said, as he walked back to his table.

The case had moved along so swiftly that Judge McIntyre was still assigned to the matter when it came up for trial. She'd handled jury selection professionally and sat quietly through opening statements.

The case had garnered more publicity the closer it had gotten to trial. Ken figured the press coverage from Judge Wexler's trial had spurred the media attention onto this case.

A thug sat in the courtroom, watching intently as the trial unfolded. The man had dark, greasy shoulder-length hair, which appeared knotted and curly. He wore a black nose ring and had visible tattoos on his exposed skin, including his wrists and neck.

Ken called Belliveau as a witness. The kid had shown up with a suit and tie and presented well. Belliveau didn't venture off script and put in the key evidence relative to an expectation of privacy in the storage locker. More importantly, he testified over objections about how he was arrested and had to pay legal fees to defend himself. He testified that he was acquitted of the crime.

The latter testimony appeared to grab the attention of all the jurors.

A person being arrested for the legal ownership of tools seemed to unsettle them. Being arrested, dragged through the criminal system, and paying legal fees, had garnered support for the plaintiff, and it provided the jury with the harm they needed to hear about.

Joey Argenziano's research had cued Ken into the fact that a person's acquittal of criminal charges can be used in the civil case. It was a game changer.

However, the defense theory that the officers acted reasonably presented a different problem, one requiring Ken to take a gamble in hope of returning a plaintiff's verdict. He just prayed it wouldn't backfire.

FORTY-FOUR

KEN called Belliveau's aunt as the next witness and she solidified the points on expectation of privacy. Boyle didn't bother to cross-examine her.

The next witness was young officer Randle. He walked to the witness box looking nervous as hell. Once he was sworn in to testify, Ken unloaded without setting up any softball questions.

"Officer Randle, you recall being deposed in this matter?" Ken said.

Boyle stood. "Objection."

"Basis?" Judge McIntyre said.

"He's leading the witness."

The judge looked at Ken. "Response?"

"Your Honor, the officer is a named party witness," Ken said. "I should have the right to treat him as a hostile witness. Besides, I don't see the question that I asked as being leading. It doesn't suppose an answer."

"You may treat him as a hostile witness and ask leading questions," Judge McIntyre said. "We don't want to be here any longer than necessary."

"Do you recall being deposed?" Ken repeated the question.

"Yes."

"You stated during your deposition that the officers involved in this matter were most concerned about letting the contraband sit, do you recall that testimony?"

"Yes, I do."

Randle looked at Ken, as if waiting for the next question, so he could explain his statement. But Ken just smiled and walked back to his table. "I am through with this witness for now, Your Honor."

Boyle was taken by surprise. He likely hadn't expected Ken would get through so many witnesses that quickly. He whispered to his colleagues. Then he faced the judge, "We do not have any questions for this witness at this time. We have listed him as a witness in the defendants' part of the case, and we reserve the right to call him then."

"Very well," Judge McIntyre looked at Ken. "Your next witness?"

"We call Officer Berwick."

***

OFFICER Berwick walked into the courtroom with his head held high. He was a burly man with sagging jowls and an arrogant demeanor. His back stood ramrod straight, his chest was out, and his chin was elevated proudly. He carried his hat under one arm, as though signifying that he never went about partially out of uniform.

Ken picked up a large stack of documents from his table and placed them on the podium.

Boyle stared at the documents with keen interest. The stack was three times the size of the discovery the defense had produced in the matter. A fervor of concerned whispers resonated from the defense table.

"Quiet down over there," Judge McIntyre said.

Boyle looked chagrined by the castigation. He pivoted towards the jury box and pretended like he hadn't been talking.

"Permission to treat the witness as hostile?" Ken said to the judge.

"You may," she replied.

"Officer Berwick, you suspected Mr. Belliveau of participating in drug trafficking, right?"

"We suspected him of being involved in pharmacy break-ins," he said. "Stealing prescription drugs. But the exact nature and extent of his involvement in drug trafficking has not yet been revealed in our investigation to date."

"You never arrested him for any drug related offense, correct?"

"Other than the charge of possession of tools related to the break-ins that you described in your opening statement, the answer is no."

"When you entered the property that is the subject of this litigation, you didn't just search the storage locker looking for tools, right?" Ken said.

"No. We searched his unit on the second floor," Berwick said. "We also searched the basement area generally, and we looked in the storage locker. As you know, Ms. Belliveau authorized the search."

A few jurors smiled at the last comment, as if recalling the sweet old lady.

"Ms. Belliveau testified that you checked kitchen cabinets, the medicine cabinet, boxes in the basement, was she correct?" Ken asked.

"Yes. I'd say so."

"Pry bars and crowbars can't fit into a medicine cabinet, can they?"

"A small crowbar might. But generally no."

"You weren't just looking for the tools seized during your search, you were trying to discover drugs?" Ken said.

"Sure. I'd say that's accurate."

"In fact you were *hoping* to find drugs, right?"

"That would have made the bust more worthwhile, sure," Berwick said. The longer he was on the stand, the more his voice sounded gruff.

"Officer Berwick," Ken said, moving closer to the witness box. "This was an ad hoc drug task force, wasn't it?"

"I guess you can say that. It wasn't formally set up by any agencies." Berwick said. "It was spearheaded by several departments working in unison. So, there were formalities to it. But not in the sense of interstate DUI task forces and drug investigations. These were break-ins we were looking into, not a drug cartel."

Several people in the courtroom snickered.

Boyle laughed out loud once he figured it was safe to do so.

"During your career," Ken continued, ignoring the chuckles. "You've heard of the term evidence shrinkage when it comes to drug cases?"

Berwick paused before answering, as if his guard had just gone up.

"Did you not hear me?" Ken said, moving closer to the witness.

"Sure. I heard you. I'm just not sure what that has to do with this case."

Boyle jumped from his chair. "Objection!"

"Basis?" the judge asked.

"Relevance."

She looked at Ken.

"I'm setting a foundation here."

"Okay, well get to it quick."

Ken nodded, then he continued. "You've heard of the term, correct?"

"Yes." Berwick looked guarded, concerned.

"You hoped to find drugs as a result of the search, right?" Ken said.

"Yes." The response was barely audible.

"You did not seek a warrant for the search, right?" Ken said.

"Correct."

"The three officers involved had a combined level of experience totaling over thirty years, right?" Ken said.

"If you say so. I'm not sure."

"There weren't any exigent circumstances when you went to the house?"

"No. But you don't need them if someone consents to the search."

"At the time of the search, you asked to look at the second-floor unit, right?"

"Correct."

"You didn't ask to look at the first-floor unit, right?" Ken said.

"No."

"That's because you suspected Mr. Belliveau lived on the second floor, right?"

"Sure, but—"

"You answered the question," Ken said. "Your lawyer can ask follow-up if he wants more detail."

Ken walked over and grabbed the first document from the stack on the podium.

Berwick eyed him carefully.

"Now, you have enough experience to know that you need the consent of the person living in the unit before you can search, right?" Ken said.

The crusty cop seemed to know that he was being baited.

Joey Argenziano had found a case that had gotten kicked when Berwick searched the closet of two college roommates. Ken held the document tightly, ready to impeach the cop.

"Yes," Berwick said, exasperated.

"You're currently going through a divorce?" Ken said.

"What's that have to do with this?" Berwick demanded.

"Objection!" Boyle bellowed. "Relevance."

Judge McIntyre looked at Ken for a response.

"Foundation."

"Go ahead."

Ken looked at Berwick for an answer.

"Yes."

Ken reached for another document. "You have several tax liens on your house, right?"

"Objection!" Boyle screamed.

Ken looked over and there was phlegm in the corner of the lawyer's mouth. Then, he glanced over at the jury. Most of them appeared to have their interest piqued.

"May we approach, Your Honor?" Ken said.

"Yes, but senior counsel only."

Ken and Boyle approached the bench for a sidebar.

"Where are you going with this?" Judge McIntyre asked Ken.

"He did the search knowing it was illegal," Ken said, "hoping to find drugs with a search that was off the books."

She nodded. Then she placed her hand over the microphone located on the edge of the bench. "I'm going to say this off the record," Judge McIntyre said. "And I'm doing so because, Mr. Boyle, you were lucky enough to draw a plaintiff's lawyer who plays well in the sandbox with others."

"Understood," Boyle said.

The judge continued to speak to Boyle. "You have an officer who just admitted on the stand that he undertook a warrantless search, and that he knew doing so was wrong at the time he conducted the search. I'm tempted to enter a directed verdict in favor of the plaintiff."

"Your Honor..." Boyle pled.

"I am going to give you a chance to settle this case. Otherwise, I'm tempted to give him wide latitude on Officer Berwick's motives. And I'll likely grant a motion for a directed verdict at the close of the plaintiff's case. You can avoid the department further embarrassment. Do I make myself clear?"

"Crystal clear," Boyle said.

"And you," she said to Ken. "Don't be greedy."

Boyle turned to Ken. "I can probably get a hundred thousand."

Ken looked at the judge. "I have to have my client's authority to settle, and he isn't the easiest person to deal with."

"Okay," Judge McIntyre said. "You go grab a conference room with your client. I'll let the jury have a break, so they aren't just sitting around."

Judge McIntyre waved for counsel to return to their tables.

"We're going to take a short recess," she announced.

FORTY-FIVE

AS THE JURY filed out of the courtroom, Ken whispered to Belliveau the defense had made a settlement offer.

Judge McIntyre told Berwick to step down from the stand, but she reminded him that he was still under oath.

"We need to go talk in a meeting room," Ken told Belliveau.

"Sure thing," Belliveau replied.

"I need to check in with opposing counsel," Ken said. "You go ahead and find us an empty room."

Belliveau nodded. Then he got up and quickly moved through the gate.

Boyle and his team were huddled near the rail, talking amongst themselves. Lieutenant O'Malley was present, and they were clearly discussing steps needed to get authority to settle.

Ken figured the case was coming to a close. He reached into his trial bag and pulled out a stack of documents. "Here you go," Ken said to Berwick, as the burly cop walked past his table.

"What's this?" Berwick griped.

"Bedtime reading. But you might want to get started on it."

Ken walked over to Boyle. "How we coming?"

Boyle nodded. "It looks good. Just don't come back too high."

As Ken headed through the gate, people in the gallery left the courtroom to check messages and use the restrooms. The thug seated in a front pew nodded at Ken with approval as the lawyer walked past.

Ken left to meet up with his client, wondering how Belliveau would respond. Money tended to talk, but this kid was a wild card.

FORTY-SIX

KEN found Belliveau in a meeting room down the hall. It had taken him a few minutes to locate the guy. Belliveau stood leaning against an oak library table.

A distrustful look was plastered on Belliveau's face; his eyes locked onto Ken when the lawyer entered the room. Belliveau traced the attorney's movements, as Ken paced in the meeting room.

The kid considered what to say and finally broke silence.

"What's the offer?" Belliveau demanded.

"They haven't confirmed it yet. But they are trying to get authority to offer you a hundred grand."

Belliveau frowned and shook his head. "No dice."

"What do you mean?" Ken said. "No dice?"

"Just what I said."

"This is a good offer," Ken said. "Cases like this are hard to win. And when you do win, they go up on appeal. You won't see any money for years."

"This isn't just about money."

Ken couldn't believe what he was hearing. This guy, a likely drug trafficker, was taking a moral high ground.

They spent half an hour discussing the merits of the case. Belliveau was convinced they would win and the defense would offer more than a hundred grand to settle after trial. Ken couldn't get through to him.

It was like a cat and mouse game, and Belliveau enjoyed having the upper hand over his lawyer. Ken intimated that maybe Belliveau might need the money.

"What's that supposed to mean?" Belliveau asked.

"I don't know," Ken said. "Maybe you are behind on child support, or have a loan."

"A loan? Who have you been talking to about this?"

"Nobody. I swear."

Belliveau seemed to be thinking. Ken figured the kid had seen the thug in the courtroom. Maybe Belliveau would come around and settle.

"You just want to get rid of me," Belliveau finally said.

"No. It's actually a good deal."

Belliveau grinned. "Even if we settle, we've got the firearms case. You're still *my* lawyer."

"Does that mean you'll take it?" Ken asked.

"No."

"What will you take?"

"A hundred and fifty grand," Belliveau said. "So long as I clear a hundred. That means your fee and expenses are capped at a third."

"Done," Ken said.

FORTY-SEVEN

RETURNING to the courtroom, Ken filled Boyle in on Belliveau's demand. Boyle walked back to the prosecution table and spoke with his team. O'Malley stood by the rail, nodding.

A moment later, Boyle stepped over to Ken's table. "We have a deal."

"Great," Ken said, smiling.

"Nice job," Boyle said, shaking Ken's hand.

Judge McIntyre noticed the celebratory behavior. "Do you have something favorable to report?"

"We have a deal," Boyle said.

"Your Honor," Ken said. "These cases involve a public entity and so confidentiality is not a concern. In fact, it's not allowed. It might make sense to take a moment to put the settlement on the record."

"Agreed," she said. "That's a great idea."

Both lawyers explained the settlement terms, which were taken down by the court stenographer. Ken noted his fee cap and how the check should be made out to his firm to hold in trust with a hundred grand owed to the plaintiff within thirty days of receiving the settlement check.

"Thank you all," Judge McIntyre said. "You may be dismissed."

"Please tell the jurors that we appreciate their time," Boyle said, winking at the judge.

"Will do."

As Ken packed up his trial bag, he noticed the sardonic grin on Belliveau's face. The kid was intolerable.

"You just got me a hundred grand," Belliveau sneered. "And I made you cut your precious fee. It's on the record. I'll clear a hundred grand."

"That's right," Ken said. "Congratulations."

"And you want to know something else?" Belliveau said.

"What?"

"Attorney/client privilege applies?" asked Belliveau.

"Yup."

"I'm guilty as sin."

***

KEN watched as Belliveau sauntered through the gate towards the exit. "Don't spend it all in one place," Ken called after Belliveau.

Berwick sidled up next to Ken. "Watch this."

Just as Belliveau reached the doors, two men and a woman in dark suits stepped from an area near the back pews.

They flashed badges. Then they placed Belliveau under arrest for firearms charges.

Federal agents placed Belliveau's hands behind his back and handcuffed him.

The gangster in the front pews watched the arrest go down with amusement.

As they led Belliveau out of the courtroom, he looked back at Ken. "You did this! You did this to me!"

Ken watched dispassionately as the agents pushed Belliveau through the door.

Berwick turned to Ken. "I don't get you Dwyer. Whose side are you on anyway?"

Ken laughed. "Not his," he said, pointing to the door. "Not anymore."

Berwick clapped Ken on the back.

Then everyone cleared out of the courtroom. Ken packed up his trial bag. He was all too happy to have the case behind him. And he was pleased to no longer be ensnared by Belliveau.

EPILOGUE

THE BAR buzzed with activity as Ken and Alyson celebrated the recent victory. Criminal defense lawyers, police, and prosecutors surrounded them. Even Boyle and his team came out for a few drinks.

Once they had a little space, Ken divulged how Belliveau had delayed getting him the firearms documents. He noticed the dates on the most recent invoices were about three years to the date of when Belliveau had turned them over.

The kid had figured he was free and clear of any statutes of limitation. However, the federal firearms regulations had five-year periods.

Ken had also figured out the invoices showed a lot of component parts. Belliveau had basically been buying receivers and components and he'd been illegally assembling assault rifles. The kid was going away for a long time.

The documents Ken had turned over to Berwick had already been produced in discovery. Ken hadn't discussed anything he'd learned through his representation of Belliveau. So, there wasn't any way for him to get into trouble over the disclosure. He was surprised how fast Berwick had figured it the issues with the gun receipts, which made Ken wonder if the feds had already been looking into Belliveau's firearms activities.

Alyson seemed pleased Ken had disclosed the information that had nabbed Belliveau. Ken planned to fill her in on the photographs with the stripper, but he thought it better to do so when the two of them were alone.

Before the festivities could get into full gear, Ken's phone buzzed. It was Mickey's wife.

Mickey was in the hospital and had suffered a stroke.

Ken took a cab over to Massachusetts General Hospital. He found Mickey and his wife in a recovery room.

Mickey smiled when Ken walked into the room. "Looks like I'm going to make it."

"Sure," Ken said. "Sure you will."

"Ken, I want you to do something for me," Mickey said.

"Whatever you need," Ken said kindly.

"Don't agree too fast."

The three of them chuckled.

"Janice, can you pass me that folder?" Mickey said. "See, we bought a place down in Florida a few months ago. We were planning to live like snowbirds for a few years then move down there year-round. But we're going to expedite things, so to speak."

"What about the firm?" Ken said.

"I've signed it over to you," Mickey said, handing over the folder. "If you'll take it."

A tear ran from the corner of the old trial lawyer's eye.

"Of course I will," Ken said. And soon tears were flowing from his eyes, too.

Then all three of them shedded tears for a moment.

Once they settled down, Mickey looked at Ken earnestly.

"What?" Ken said.

"As you can expect," Mickey replied. "There is just a small kicker in there for me and my family."

"I wouldn't have it any other way," Ken said, laughing.

ABOUT THE STORY

The genesis for this story came from an assignment in law school. I had taken a class in Constitutional Law/Criminal Procedure. The professor was a Superior Court judge, who taught the class as part of the law school's adjunct faculty.

An assignment he had given the class was to write a motion to suppress based upon an actual case. We received pleadings and police report from the case. It involved a search and seizure of tools used in suspected pharmacy break-ins that had occurred in Massachusetts and New Hampshire. No drugs were found, but the police had uncovered pry bars and other tools associated with such break-ins. My position taken in the class was the items subject to the warrantless search should be suppressed. The professor seemed to agree.

ABOUT THE AUTHOR

John W. Dennehy is the author of the thrillers *Limited Damages, Arraigned,* and others. After graduating from Pinkerton Academy, he enlisted in the U.S. Marines. He graduated from UNC Wilmington and Suffolk Law. John was a Litigation Partner at a Boston law firm for many years. He is a member of International Thriller Writers. He lives in New Hampshire and can be found at his website: http://johnwdennehy.com/

Made in the USA
Middletown, DE
09 January 2024

47518566R00115